Dear Emma

JOHANNA HURWITZ

Dear Emma

ILLUSTRATED BY
BARBARA GARRISON

HARPERCOLLINS*PUBLISHERS*

Dear Emma

Copyright © 2002 by Johanna Hurwitz

For information address HarperCollins Children's Books, a division of HarperCollins Publishers, 1350 Avenue of the Americas, New York, NY 10019.

www.harperchildrens.com

Library of Congress Cataloging-in-Publication Data

Hurwitz, Johanna.

    Dear Emma / Johanna Hurwitz ; illustrated by Barbara Garrison.

    p. cm.

    Sequel to: Faraway summer.

    Summary: In her letters to a Vermont friend, eighth grader Dossi, a Russian, Jewish immigrant living in the Lower East Side of New York City in 1910, shares her thoughts about her new brother-in-law, the diphtheria epidemic, and the Triangle Shirtwaist Factory fire.

    ISBN 0-06-029840-5 — ISBN 0-06-029841-3 (lib. bdg.)

    [1. Immigrants—Fiction. 2. Jews—New York (N.Y.)—Fiction. 3. Orphans—Fiction. 4. Russian Americans—Fiction. 5. New York (N.Y.)—History—1898–1951—Fiction. 6. Letters—Fiction.] I. Garrison, Barbara, ill. II. Title.

PZ7.H9574 Dc 2002   2002001466

[Fic]—dc21   CIP

                                          AC

Typography by Andrea Vandergrift

1 2 3 4 5 6 7 8 9 10

First Edition

For Nomi

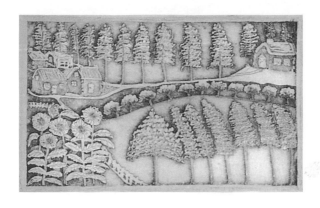

August 17, 1910

Dear Mr. and Mrs. Meade,

Yesterday, when I returned home from my two-week stay at your house, there was a postcard waiting for me from the Fresh Air Fund. The card directed me to write and thank you for your generosity in opening your home to a stranger.

As if I needed to be told to thank you! As if I hadn't already told you how I felt. But one can never thank someone too much for an act of kindness. So here is my letter to you.

I must confess that I was nervous and frightened when I arrived at your home. Rural country life in Vermont is so different from the crowded Lower

East Side of New York City that I felt as if I had arrived on the other side of the world. But your warm welcome soon made me forget to be homesick. You know that I will never forget those days we spent together. I confess that now I feel homesick for *you,* my Vermont family. If I close my eyes and concentrate hard, I can still taste your wonderful homemade bread and butter and smell the freshly cut hay and the pine trees outside your house.

Please tell Emma that I will soon write a long letter to her. Tell Nell that I haven't forgotten my promise to write to her as well. Tell Edward and Timothy that I miss them, too. Will you believe me if I say I even miss the cows?

My very best wishes to all the family, and again thank you so very much for your kindness and generosity to me.

Fondly,
Hadassah (Dossi) Rabinowitz

Silvester Building, New York.

August 27, 1910

Dear Nell,

Here it is: the first piece of mail addressed to you.
I promised that I would send you something and now
you can see that I keep my word. Never again can you
complain that no one has ever written to you.

The picture on this card shows you one tiny little
piece of New York City. Perhaps someday you will
visit here, but you will not see this building. It was
demolished this year, and so this little card is actually
a piece of history. Never mind, there is so much more
that I can show you.

Your friend,
Dossi

Dear Emma,

I had planned to write to you the very moment that I arrived home. However, I have been very busy, and today is the first chance that I've had to sit quietly and describe all that has occurred in my life since we said good-bye to each other.

My train ride passed without any problems. As it was my second such trip (the first, of course, was going to visit you), I was now an experienced traveler. But when I was traveling to Jericho, Vermont, I was so nervous that I wished the train would move more slowly. I didn't know then that we would become good friends! Going home, even though I was sorry to leave you, I was eager to see my sister. Ruthi is all the family I have, and my time with you was our first separation.

Somehow the same number of miles going home seemed to take twice as long as when I traveled in the other direction.

You may remember that, while I was in Jericho, I received a letter from my sister announcing that she was engaged to be married. So when I finally arrived at the train station in New York, I wasn't too surprised to see her accompanied by Meyer Reisman, her future husband. The surprise, however, was their news. Instead of waiting to get married in the winter as they had originally planned, they have decided to get married in two weeks.

As they excitedly told me their plans, I saw that much had changed in just the couple of weeks that I was away. Ruthi was wearing a new dress. Her long hair was combed back and pinned up on her head in a more stylish manner than I'd ever seen before. As for my soon-to-be brother-in-law, I had met him a few times in the past. He had a dark beard that covered much of his face, but on the top of his head the hair is growing thin. The short, stocky man waiting beside my sister at the train platform was clean shaven. It actually took me a moment to recognize Meyer. Then at once I began to worry. I never knew that, under his beard, Meyer has a dimple in his chin. I have heard rumored more than once that men or women with such a dimple lose their first wife or husband. And that is exactly what happened to Meyer. His first wife died in childbirth. I know that Ruthi should be safe because she will be the second wife. But somehow I began to feel very nervous around Meyer. Did he have a beard when he wed his first wife? Did she know that she was doomed? And what other bad luck does Meyer bring with him, I wondered.

Still, Meyer tried hard to please me. He embraced me and called me "sister." Then he took my valise and offered to buy me a glass of Coca Cola from a stand in the station. I confess, I had never tasted this drink because I have never had five cents to squander for such a thing. I agreed at once. I might not have the offer again, I thought. Have you ever had Coca Cola? It's a dark color and cold and sweet to the taste. But there is a funny bubbly quality to the drink that I didn't expect. Almost at once, the bubbles got up my nose and I coughed and came close to spilling my glass. Ruthi caught it in time and took a sip.

"Dossi and I are accustomed to water," she told Meyer.

When we finished the drink, we continued on our way, taking the trolley downtown to our home. (In case you've never seen one, a trolley is a little like a train in that it rides on a track. It is powered by electricity and is only one car long. People can get off and on as it travels along the streets.) It all looked so strange. I was away only two weeks and already my eyes had forgotten how crowded the city is. And as we left the more prosperous area uptown and got closer to home, the crowds of people, horse-drawn wagons and carts, peddlers, and noise kept growing more and more. Meanwhile Ruthi was busy telling me the news as fast as she could—which neighbor had a baby, what acquaintance was sick, the gifts Meyer's relatives wanted to give her, and what had happened here while I was away. The biggest piece of news was that the mayor of New York City, Mr. Gaynor, was shot and almost killed as he was boarding a ship to take a vacation. Now he is in the hospital and the reports say he is likely to recover. But this incident made me realize how very fortunate I was. Though I am but a poor, humble girl, and not a wealthy and important person, I was returning from a wonderful vacation.

And then I was really home again. Ruthi and I have been living in a small room that is within the apartment of a family named Aronson. Can you believe that two people can live in a single room? Actually we're very lucky. There are some people who live with eight or ten crowded into a room. The Aronsons use our bit of rent money to pay some of their bills, and in exchange they permit us to use the stove in their kitchen and the privy in the hallway outside of the apartment. When Ruthi and Meyer are married, I will move with Ruthi to his larger apartment. I will describe it in my next letter.

Meyer had scarcely put my valise down in a corner of the room when there was a knock on our door. It was my friend Mimi. We embraced, delighted to see each another again. Then Mimi and I sat on the two chairs that Ruthi and I own. Ruthi took our kettle into the Aronsons' kitchen to boil some water for tea. When she returned, she exclaimed, "Oh, Dossi. I knew I forgot something. I was going to buy some cake to welcome you home."

"I am welcomed without cake," I said. Then, seeing a loaf of bread on the table, I jumped up and began slicing it. "I have a surprise," I told them. I went to my valise and removed the jar of strawberry preserves that your mother had sent home with me. I spread the jam on the slices of bread and we ate it with our cups of tea. Emma, please be sure and tell your mother. It was better than cake.

Your friend in New York City,
Dossi

Dear Emma,

Thank you for the beautiful leaves that you sent me. They arrived in perfect condition. I had heard of the magnificence of the autumn in New England and now I can say that I, too, have seen the red and golden leaves. Perhaps someday I will have the opportunity to see the colored leaves while they are still attached to the branches of the trees.

I'm glad to know that Rural Free Delivery has just begun in your community and now mail will be delivered right to your home. You won't have the long walk to the post office to see if I've written you another letter. Our mail here is delivered to our tenement building. And the first thing I look for when I return from school is a new letter from you.

So very much has happened since my last letter. You say that you and Nell have begun the new semester at school. So have I. Now I'm in the eighth grade. At the end of the year, I'll have to decide which high school I will attend and if I'll take a course of study to prepare me for college. That is my dream.

The new school year is only a small part of what has occurred in my life. First of all there was the wedding. It was not like the fancy affairs that we read about in the novels we borrow from the library. Instead, it took place in the study of a local rabbi. (A rabbi is the Jewish equivalent of a minister.) Ruthi wore still another new dress. It was the color of the cream from one of your cows. Meyer wore a dark blue suit and cravat. They both looked elegant and very happy. Meyer's closest relatives, an elderly aunt and uncle, were there. Although they have lived in this country for many years, they speak very little English. Mostly they talk to each other and their nephew in German. However, as Ruthi and I used to speak Yiddish with our parents (Yiddish is a Jewish language that is derived from German and contains many Hebrew words as well), we could partially

adj : being, possessing

understand this couple when they spoke. In fact, we probably understood more than they first realized. I overheard Mrs. Reisman say, "She's very pretty but so pale and thin." She was talking about Ruthi, and hearing her, my sister was no longer pale but blushed a deep red. A friend of Meyer's named David was there, and Ruthi's friend Rosa from the shirtwaist factory managed to come, too. In addition, there were a few of the rabbi's students who served as witnesses. Ruthi and Meyer stood under a canopy made of dark blue velvet and decorated with gold silk embroidery. The canopy is called a *chuppah* and it is part of Jewish tradition. When our parents were wed in the old country, they, too, stood under a *chuppah*. The ceremony was brief and in Hebrew, so I couldn't actually understand what was said.

A covering, usually of cloth

Afterward we (the elder Reismans, Ruthi, Meyer, Rosa, David, and I) walked to 14th Street to F. W. Woolworth & Co., which is a large store that sells every possible item you could ever want to buy, as well as many you will never want, too. Mimi and I have gone there a few times. We just like to look around and stare at the merchandise, which is arranged on big countertops throughout the store. Only a few days before the wedding, the Woolworth store added an area where one can take a meal. It is called the Refreshment Room. There are sixteen tables (I counted) with marble tops and a huge food counter displaying what you can order. Everywhere there are fresh flowers, so you quickly forget that you are in the midst of the city. Instead, it seems as if one is in a garden. Uniformed waiters and waitresses serve the food on fine china dishes. So even if the wedding ceremony was performed in a shabby room, the elegance of this place was more than I could ever imagine.

I felt like a princess out of a storybook sitting there. I could see that Rosa did, too.

"Isn't this beautiful," she whispered to me. "It must be what it looks like in paradise."

I was glad that Rosa was enjoying herself. Ruthi had told me that her friend was losing a whole day's wages just so she could join the wedding party. Ruthi said sometimes workers are fired if they miss a day of work, but Rosa is such a good seamstress that her position at the factory was not at risk.

"Such an expense," said Meyer's aunt, looking around. "I could have prepared a meal for you."

"This is a celebration," Meyer said. "I didn't want you to work today. Besides, there is nothing served here that costs over ten cents." After that, I kept busy adding figures in my head. The cost of my glass of milk and slice of strudel pastry and the glasses of beer that the men drank and the little sandwiches that Ruthi and Rosa nibbled on. I am sure Meyer had to pay more than three dollars just for our light meal. But to tell you the truth, I agree with him. It was a celebration and it was worth every penny he spent.

While we were eating our food, I turned to my new brother to ask him the question that had been troubling me. "Why did you shave off your beard?" I inquired.

He laughed. "I wondered that you didn't ask me before," he said. "I didn't shave for a year after Sylvia (that was his first wife) and the baby died," he explained. "And then I became accustomed to living behind that beard of mine. One day Ruthi commented that she couldn't see who I was. So I cut the beard off. I guess I must look like a new person to you. And to tell the truth, I feel like a new person as well." He turned and smiled at my sister. It is wonderful to see her so happy, though I do wish our parents were alive to share this time. I remain suspicious of Meyer and his dimpled chin. But I won't say anything to Ruthi. How can I spoil her great joy?

The only thing that upset my pleasure during the lunch party was a comment in German from Meyer's aunt. I heard her say to her husband, "Why does Meyer need two women? One wife should satisfy any man." I'm not sure what she meant. Is Ruthi the second woman? Or is it me?

I think I told you that Meyer is a pharmacist. That means he has a very good job and gets a fine weekly paycheck. As a result, he has been able to afford to rent a whole apartment in a tenement building for himself without sharing it with others. (Tenements are buildings of four or five stories. Inside are groups of rooms called apartments, and sometimes a dozen people can live in one such apartment. There may be as many people living in Meyer's tenement building as there are living within many miles of your home.)

When we first arrived in America from Russia, we shared an apartment with some cousins of my mother's. I can barely remember them, and now they've moved to another part of the country. After Papa died, we saved money by moving to a single room in another apartment. And still later, when Ruthi and I were alone, we lived in a smaller room. If Ruthi is unhappy because now she's living in the same three rooms where Meyer lived with his deceased wife, she doesn't mention it. This is the first time since we've come to America that we don't have to share our space with other people. Meyer has given Ruthi money so that she can buy fabric to make new curtains and get whatever else she feels we need. Ruthi is happiest about the small kitchen that she can use whenever she wants. Never again will she have to ask Mrs. Aronson if it's convenient for her to boil some water or to make a pot of soup for us. In addition to the kitchen, there's a tiny bed-room for Ruthi and Meyer and a larger sitting room we all use.

There's a bed for me in one corner of this room. Meyer put some nails into the wall so I can hang my dresses on them, and I've a little chest for storing my undergarments and other small things. Ruthi is going to make a curtain to put around my area so that I can have a little privacy. (And Meyer and Ruthi will have privacy, too, if they sit at the table in the evening after I'm in bed.) The curtain will make my corner really seem like a room of my own. When I have homework or want to write a letter, I can either sit at the table in the center of the sitting room where we eat our meals, or I can sit on my bed and lean upon a book.

There was an old piece of cracked and stained linoleum on the floor near my bed. It looked very ugly, and I asked for permission to remove it. "I'd rather see the bare wood of the floor than this old linoleum," I told Meyer.

"Do as you wish," he told me. "It's your space."

Amazingly, I discovered a hole in the floor under the linoleum. Some previous tenant had stuffed the hole with an old rag. I pulled it up and out of it fell many coins and even some bills. It added up to more than ten dollars. I ran to give this treasure to Ruthi and Meyer.

"It's yours," Meyer said. "I never saw it before and you found it."

"But shouldn't we try and locate the previous tenant?" I asked.

"I've lived here for three years," Meyer reminded me. "It would be like looking for a needle in a haystack. Besides, perhaps it belonged to a tenant prior to the last tenant. Anyone would be happy to claim that money as theirs."

I could see his point. And so suddenly I became amazingly rich. Now I won't have to beg coins from Ruthi to buy the stamps to put on my letters to you.

I was afraid it would be awkward for me living

with Meyer. Ruthi and I had been together and on our own for so long. But I must say Meyer is a true gentleman. He calls me his little sister and includes me in his conversations with Ruthi. However, the other evening when he and Ruthi were going to a free concert at Cooper Union and Ruthi invited me to join them, I could see in his face that this had not been Meyer's plan. I would certainly have enjoyed attending a concert, but I had the good sense to know that my brother-in-law would be much happier without me tagging along. So I told them I had a lot of homework. I didn't, but I did have a new library book waiting to be read, and so I stayed here in our apartment.

By the way, I paid for the copy of *Anne of Green Gables* that was left out in the rain during the summer. Is it my imagination, or does the librarian look at me suspiciously whenever I check out a book these days?

In addition to my library books, I have something new to read. Each morning Meyer buys a newspaper on his way to work. "Does so much happen in the world that you need to spend a penny every single day?" I asked in surprise when he brought home his paper for the fourth day in a row.

"Much more happens in the world than can ever be contained in a single newspaper," Meyer replied. "I am fascinated by the world around me. But I am also very interested in what is close to me," he said, smiling at Ruthi.

So now most evenings when I have finished my schoolwork, I turn to Meyer's newspaper. *The New York Times* is filled with stories of what is happening in the city and all over the country and even all over the world. There are many calamities: fires, murders, diseases, sinking ships, suicides. One could get very distressed were it not for the good news, too. I read all sorts of things. Now I know the price of renting a new apartment uptown, I know which books are being sold, what operas and plays are being performed, and what styles are in fashion. I can never finish reading everything in the newspaper, and the next day there is another one when Meyer comes home from the pharmacy. In the past, Ruthi and I never spent our money on a newspaper, but I can remember my father reading a Yiddish paper when I was small. He even began to teach me some of the Hebrew letters before he became ill.

For Jewish people like me, a New Year began on October 4th. So here I am in a New Year with a new home, a new brother, and a new fortune. What else will this year bring?

Your very rich friend,
Dossi

P.S. The library book that I read is *The Casting Away of Mrs. Lecks and Mrs. Aleshine* by Frank Stockton. It's very funny. Have you read it?

November 11, 1910

Dear Emma, and hello to Nell, too,

When I got your letter dated October 18th, I was amazed to learn that your house and land were deeply covered by snow. We here can expect our share of snow when winter comes to this part of the world. But it's unlikely that we'll have snow before mid-December. You said that sometimes you have snow even in April. What long winters you have in Vermont!

In fact, while you were helping your brothers dig a path to the barn and bringing in wood for your stove and fireplace, it was so warm here that Mimi and I decided to have an all-day outing. We took a trolley all the way uptown to Central Park. I'd been to the park a few times before, but this time we did something special. We went to the Menagerie. Can you imagine, there's an area inside the park with large wooden sheds that house lions, tigers, jaguars, monkeys, black bears, and a camel. My favorite were the pair of elephants. They look just like the drawings in my geography book at school, with huge dark bodies and long trunks and tusks. A sign told us their names: Jewel and Hattie.

Mimi laughed and laughed when she read the sign. "My grandmother is named Hattie, just like that elephant," she said. I laughed, too, when I heard that.

After we spent a long time wandering through the zoo, we sat on a bench and ate the apples and bread and cheese we'd brought with us for our lunch. We watched the people coming and going, parents pushing infants in perambulators, nursemaids wearing starched uniforms caring for young children, and gentlemen escorting women along the park paths. Everyone seemed to be enjoying themselves, but none more than Mimi and I. It is rare for us to go off on an adventure.

Poor Mimi has a great deal of responsibility at

home, helping her mother take care of her younger sisters and brothers. And of course we both have to do our homework for school.

Also, of course, I have been working to adjust to my new life. I should have no complaints now that I am living in roomier quarters with a space all my own, a warm meal every day instead of just once a week, and money in my pocket for small extravagances. But I realize now that having been an orphan for two years and living with Ruthi, who was away for long hours at work, made me very independent. However, since she became a married woman, Ruthi no longer goes off to work. Instead, she stays home and cleans the apartment, cooks our meals, does the laundry, mends, and watches me. "Where are you going?" she asks whenever I leave the apartment. "When will you be back?" she wants to know. I'm not accustomed to so much supervision. And it is not just from Ruthi. Meyer, too, wants me to account for my every move.

The day Mimi and I went to the zoo, we didn't return home until after sundown, because we walked all the way home. We were very tired but pleased with ourselves for saving the fare. And besides, it was lovely to have such a long visit together, talking all the way and discussing the people and sights that we saw. But when I got home, Ruthi and Meyer were angry.

"Where were you?" Ruthi demanded to know.

"Where did you think?" I asked her. "Do you suppose I went to the moon? You knew that I was going to Central Park with Mimi. You knew I'd come home again."

"But it's so late," she said. "It's so dark."

"I'm not afraid of the dark," I told her.

"We're responsible for you," Meyer said. "And young girls shouldn't be out alone at this hour."

"You're not my father," I yelled at him. "I'm twelve years old, almost thirteen. I don't need to be watched like a baby!"

Meyer stomped off angrily into their bedroom.

Ruthi took me aside and scolded me. She reminded me that the food I eat and the rent for the apartment is paid for by her husband. "You must respect him," she told me. I was about to say that I didn't take any marriage vow to honor and obey him, but I bit back my words. I don't want to make Ruthi and her husband have fights about me. And so later that evening, I apologized to Meyer, and we are again on good terms. I hope it will last. But in the meantime, those angry words with Ruthi and Meyer took away some of the pleasure from my day with Mimi. It didn't make me feel better to hear that Mimi's mother scolded her as well.

It's not just me that Meyer is watching. He came home from work early, hoping to surprise Ruthi, and discovered her sweeping the hallway and stairs outside of our apartment. "You don't need to do that," he insisted.

"Oh, Meyer. If I don't, no one will," she protested.

"I won't have my wife cleaning up after other people," he said, referring to some of our neighbors who drop their garbage as they're carrying it out to the street. Often someone will toss an apple core, nut shells, or the butt end of a cigarette as they walk past our door. They seem to have no sense of what is right and what isn't.

Ruthi looked over at me, and I knew she was worried that I might reveal that she does much more than just sweep the hallway. Almost every day she washes out the communal privy, which is a much dirtier job. But the truth is someone has to do it, and I'm relieved to walk in and find it clean. I didn't give away her secret.

"What about when we have children?" Ruthi asked Meyer. "I'll be cleaning up after them and they will be *other* people."

"I won't have my wife cleaning up after people who are not our family," he said, amending his earlier statement. But I realized that Ruthi had cleverly distracted him. I know their dream is to become parents.

Our neighbors are not all so slovenly in their habits as you might suppose from what I wrote. Just below us on the second floor lives a widow with two young girls: Becky and Bluma Edelman. They are three and four years old. Both have dark brown eyes and curly brown hair and big smiles. Sometimes I watch after them when their mother is busy.

Becky and Bluma like to sit on the bed in my little corner and listen to me make up stories. Often I cut paper dolls for them. It's something that my mother did for me when I was small. But Becky and Bluma's favorite activity is cuddling Sadie, my old rag doll who sits on the top of the chest near my bed. My mother made the doll for Ruthi, who passed her on to me when I was Bluma's age. Mama made Sadie from an old sheet, and she used bits of an old skirt to make her a dress. Her eyes are a pair of buttons and her nose and mouth are stitched onto her face. Originally, Sadie had brown hair made from knitting wool. But when she became my doll, Mama cut off all her hair and gave her a new hairdo. Using bright red wool, Mama gave Sadie red hair to match mine. By now, you can imagine, this doll is quite worn. She was played with in a hundred games, first by Ruthi and then by me. But every stitch on her body was put there by my mother's hands, and except for a couple of family photographs and a brooch that Ruthi wears, there is nothing else left of our mother except memories.

"Can Sadie come downstairs to visit in our house?" Bluma begs me each time I go to her apartment.

"No, Sadie will miss me too much," I tell her. "But you can visit her upstairs whenever you want."

That seems to satisfy her. And if I were a better seamstress, I would try and make a pair of dolls for the sisters. But since I can't, I keep them occupied with the paper dolls that I make. We draw different faces on them—smiling, sad, and even asleep with their eyes closed.

As I write this letter, my eyes are wishing to close,

too. So I will end here and go to sleep. Good night, Emma. "Happy dreams," as my mama used to always tell me.

Your friend,
Dossi

P.S. This month I read two books by Gene Stratton-Porter. They are *Freckles* and *Girl of the Limberlost.* Both of them are excellent, although they made me cry.

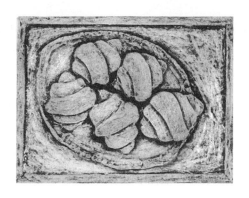

Dear Emma,

I was so surprised to get your last letter and to
learn that you don't need to go to a Menagerie to see
black bears. I never guessed that some are roaming
in the woods of Vermont. I am certain that I would
have been very nervous if I had thought a bear might
walk out of the woods when we were berry picking
last summer. Thank you for not telling me about it
then. But you didn't mention elephants or camels in
your letter, so I guess New York City does have a few
new sights in store for you if you ever visit here.

Can you tell from my handwriting or my language
that I am no longer twelve years old? My birthday

was last week. Ruthi baked some pastries like my mother used to make to celebrate the occasion. We didn't have the money to buy the ingredients for a long time, and I had forgotten all about these little cakes called *rugelach*. (It's pronounced rug-a-lach.) It was a wonderful surprise to come home from school and smell them baking in the oven. It almost made me cry because it smelled as if my mama was cooking in our kitchen. The pastries are so delicious that I would love to send some to you, but I am afraid they might not travel well in the mail and all you would receive is a box of crumbs. So I shall enclose the recipe. Perhaps one day you and Nell and your mother might want to make them and think of me as you savor their taste.

To celebrate my birthday, Mimi's mother permitted her to come home from school with me and stay until it got dark. She brought her jumping rope and we went outdoors. Before long, several other girls in the neighborhood joined us. We took turns with two holding the ends of the rope while the rest of us jumped. Bluma and Becky sat on the steps in front of our building watching. They haven't yet mastered the skill of this game.

"Someday soon, I'll teach you how to do this, too," I promised them.

Still, they found it entertaining enough just to watch us big girls, though it must have been cold for them to sit still. Mimi and I were kept warm by our jumping.

When Mimi and I went back upstairs, Ruthi had a birthday surprise waiting for me. It was a new dress, which she had been secretly sewing while I was at school each day. Meyer gave me a book. It is the Funk & Wagnalls *Abridged Dictionary*. So now there will be no excuse for misspelled words in my letters to you. I must secretly confess that, useful as a dictionary is, I would rather have a book with a story in it. But of course I thanked Meyer graciously. It was kind of him to give me a gift of any sort.

Mimi gave me a pair of handkerchiefs, which she had hidden in her schoolbag. She had hemmed them herself and embroidered my initials, *HR,* with red thread on one and blue thread on the other. Mimi is an excellent seamstress. Her birthday is in April, and she's been talking about leaving school at the end of the school year. At thirteen she will be able to get work in one of the garment factories. I know her family needs money, as her father does not earn very much and there are five children to feed and clothe. But I hope she can continue her education.

"I can read and write. That's more than my mother can do," she says when I urge her to remain in school.

"But you'll have a better future with more education," I remind her.

"When I am a housewife someday, it won't matter if I can do difficult arithmetic problems or recite Latin verbs and Shakespearean sonnets," she says. I know she's right. But she's wrong, too. I want to go to high school and even to college. One can never learn too much. Still, I know that Mimi's arguments are not to me. She is telling herself that school doesn't matter because she is afraid she must leave. There are evening classes for working people, but after ten hours of sewing in a factory, it's hard to stay awake and study. Supper and bed is what the laborer wants when the day's work is completed.

Many, many of the women in our area work in garment factories. If you counted all of them and their output, you would think that all the clothing in the world is made in this neighborhood. Ruthi used to be employed at the Triangle Shirtwaist Factory. Once

I went to meet her at the end of the day, and her boss permitted her to show me the place where she sat and sewed. ("He's counting on you coming to work here one of these days," Ruthi whispered to me. "But I hope you never have to.")

Hundreds of women work there, side by side, for ten long, long hours a day. The air is hot and thick with lint from the fabric on which they are sewing and cutting patterns. Ruthi says that sometimes it is hard to breathe. Many of the women cough while they work. They spit into handkerchiefs or even onto the floor. After a while, the job is so automatic for them that they are able to speak and sew at the same time. Most of the women employed by the factory are Jewish or Italian. When they were all working hard and feeling tired, national and religious backgrounds were forgotten. They were all the same.

And that's why Ruthi's closest friend in the factory was Rosa, even though Ruthi (like me) was born in Russia and Rosa comes from Italy. "Ruthi and Rosa," the others always said. "Rosa and Ruthi." First they discovered that they shared the same birth month and day, although Rosa is two years older than Ruthi.

Soon they shared their lunches and their life stories, too. "I feel as if I know Rosa as well as I know you," Ruthi once told me.

Last spring there was a workers' strike. The girls and women in the factory were making only three or four dollars for working ten hours a day, six days a week. (Men and boys are always paid more than women.)

"It is totally unfair," Ruthi told me, and I certainly agreed with her.

So there was much talk about everyone staying home from work as a protest to the factory owners. When it was still being planned, Ruthi and Rosa kept trying to make up their minds about whether or not to take part. On days when Rosa said they should strike, Ruthi would ask, "What happens if we lose our jobs?" And then when Rosa agreed they had better not strike, Ruthi would say, "If we don't complain together, we will never make more money than we do now."

"Go ahead and strike," I told Ruthi firmly.

"It's easy for you to say that," she responded. "What will we eat when I don't make any money?"

I didn't have an answer, but I knew if Ruthi and

her coworkers didn't strike, the situation would never improve. In the end, Ruthi and Rosa decided to just keep on working. But they both felt bad for not supporting this effort. And when the strike was over, the workers returned to their jobs without much change in their salaries or working conditions.

"See, it didn't matter," Ruthi said to me. "And I didn't lose any wages like those striking women did."

But it did matter. The women who had stayed home from work resented those who had continued working. And this drew Ruthi and Rosa even closer together.

Rosa is taller than my sister, but her posture is stooped from sitting over a sewing machine for so many hours a week. She began working at the factory when she was twelve, so she has spent more time there than Ruthi. Rosa has dark black hair and a wonderful laugh. But even though she loves to joke and laugh, life has been even harder for Rosa than for others. She lives with a married brother and his wife and children. When she smiles or laughs, you can't help noticing that she has lost two of her front teeth.

Ruthi was so delighted when Rosa came to her

wedding celebration. Rosa does not have many parties in her life. Because Rosa works such long hours, they have not seen each other since that day. I know Ruthi is very happy not to have to work in the factory. She says that perhaps she will take some piecework to do at home and earn a little money that way. But Meyer is proud of his ability to support the three of us. So I suspect he will discourage Ruthi from doing this.

In a way, my friendship with you is like that of Ruthi and Rosa. We come from different backgrounds, but now we are growing to be like sisters. And like them, we don't see each other. But I am luckier than Ruthi. I can look forward to fat letters from you with your interesting descriptions of life in Jericho. I love what you wrote about Nell chasing the chickens, and I imagine the cows with the steam coming from their mouths now that the weather is cold. All those cows need are cigars to make them look like some of the men I've seen around here. (There are factories nearby where men roll the tobacco into cigars all day long. That must be just as boring as the constant sewing.)

Ruthi does not get letters from Rosa or see her.

When she finishes her long day of work at the factory, Rosa has to help her brother's wife take care of their three children. So there is no time for visiting. And Ruthi told me one of Rosa's secrets. Rosa cannot read or write. To me that is the worst thing of all—worse than working all day, worse than being poor, worse than losing teeth. Imagine how terrible it would be not to read any books!

I have seen advertisements for telephones in Meyer's newspaper. It seems that more and more (rich) people are having them installed in their homes. There is a telephone in the pharmacy where Meyer works. Meyer says it is very useful because doctors call and order medicines, which can then be prepared and ready for the patient. Meyer also says that he believes in time telephones will become so common and cheap that everyone will have one in their home. I can't believe it. Can you? But wouldn't it be wonderful if he was right? Then I could hear your voice and you could hear mine. People like Rosa could use the telephone and speak with their old friends even if they haven't time to visit with them. I am sure this is a fantasy, though.

Write soon and tell me more about winter in

Vermont. And tell me what books you are reading, too.

Your friend,
Dossi

P.S. This month I've been rereading some old favorites by Louisa May Alcott.

Mama & Ruthi's Rugelach Recipe

1) Make dough using one cup of softened butter and one cup of softened cream cheese. Mix with two cups of flour and a pinch of salt.

2) When the dough is made, knead it like you are making bread until all the ingredients are well combined. Wrap with a piece of cloth and put it into the icebox or a cool place until the dough hardens.

3) Divide the hardened dough into four parts. Roll out until the dough is about 1/8 inch thick.

4) Cut each circle of dough into a dozen or more triangles, as though you are slicing a pie.

5) Sprinkle raisins or currants and chopped walnuts, all of which have been mixed with a little cinnamon and sugar, into the center of each piece of dough. Roll up dough starting at the wide end and moving toward the tip. (Rugelach can also be filled with jam mixed with chopped nuts.)

6) Place rugelach on a greased baking pan and put into a medium oven. Bake for about 20–25 minutes until lightly brown and done.

7) Eat!

Dear Emma,

This will be my last letter to you written in 1910. I couldn't wait until the New Year to thank you for the wonderful parcels that arrived here for all of us. Jewish people do not celebrate Christmas or exchange Christmas gifts. But one does not need to be a Christian to enjoy receiving a present. Ruthi and Meyer and I will savor every mouthful of the raspberry and blackberry jams that you helped your mother prepare. We already finished eating the delicious fruitcake. Thank you so much. But most of all I want to thank you for the special present you made for me.

When I opened the bulky package, I couldn't imagine what you had sent. I cannot tell you how excited I was when I saw the rag rug. It's both useful and beautiful! I could even identify some of the fabric scraps: a bit of the print dresses you and Nell wore last summer and a piece of your mother's apron. The rug is now on the floor in front of my bed. It feels wonderful to put my bare feet down on it instead of on the cold and splintery wooden floor. I will think of you every morning when I wake up and again when I get into bed at night. So thank you, thank you, thank you for all the generous gifts you sent.

I'm afraid that the package I mailed did not have a high monetary value. But I do hope it arrived safely. What it lacked in value was made up for by the affection that it carried to you and your family. I worked knitting those woolen mittens for you and Nell all during the autumn. Ruthi is always knitting and crocheting, but in the past I didn't have the patience to sit still and do the same thing. Perhaps it's a sign I'm getting older that I was able to start a project and finish it in time. Ruthi helped me make the thumbs, and she picked up my dropped stitches, too. I'll imagine you and Nell walking or playing in the snow wearing those mittens. I hope they keep you warm. I also hope that your family enjoys looking at the album of postcards that I assembled with pictures of New York. It's my plan to send more cards during the year that can be added to the album. Then you'll be able to visualize the city where I live. But someday you'll have to come here to see and hear and smell the city. Where I live, there are people speaking Yiddish, Italian, German, Russian, and of course English with a variety of accents. The pushcart vendors shout out to urge you to stop and buy their wares. There is always a lot of noise! Also, if you walked along Houston Street with me, you could smell the pickles in the barrels filled with brine, fresh and smoked fish, half-plucked chickens and geese, newly baked bread, dried fruit, and a hundred other things.

I confess that not all the odors are good ones. In many of the tenement buildings, one can smell urine (forgive me, but it's true). There are also the cooking smells of cabbage, potatoes, onions, fried fish, coffee, and whatever else is being prepared inside each apartment. I am so accustomed to these sounds and smells that I only half notice them. But to you they'd probably be overwhelming, and you would

want to hurry home to the serenity and the fragrance
of the meadows surrounding your house.

Your friend,
Dossi

Flat Iron Building, New York

New York Public Library, New York

Union Square, New York

Bowery Street, New York

Swan Pond, Central Park, New York

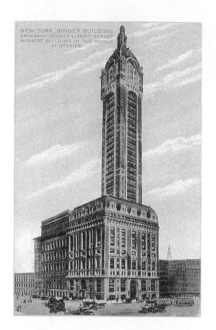

Singer Building, New York

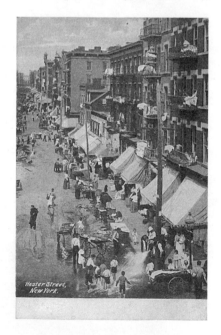

Hester Street, New York

January 6, 1911

Dear Emma,

I am ashamed to confess that I began the new year with a big fight with Meyer. Yesterday afternoon I was sitting at our table with all my school papers around me. When Meyer returned from work, I was doing an exercise in algebra, which is not my favorite subject. I looked up as he entered the apartment and nodded to him. I had just grasped the concept that the teacher had explained several times at school and wanted to apply it to one of the problems.

"Why are you just sitting there while your sister is working?" Meyer demanded.

I was startled by his words. I looked over toward

the kitchen, where Ruthi was standing at the stove. Her hair was coming out of its bun and her face was flushed. Usually she washes her face and combs her hair before Meyer arrives.

"Why don't you help Ruthi sometimes instead of reading books and entertaining yourself?" Meyer asked.

By then Ruthi had left the stove to defend me. "Dossi is doing her school assignment," she pointed out. "That's her work."

"She should help you first. Then she can do her schoolwork."

At that I gathered up my arithmetic book and all of my papers. I flung them on my bed and grabbed my coat off its nail. "Don't you tell me what to do!" I shouted to Meyer as I rushed to the door. I looked at Ruthi and announced, "I'm not staying here with him."

I slammed the door behind me and ran down the stairs. At the bottom landing, I waited to hear if Ruthi would come after me. She didn't. I went out into the street. It was almost six o'clock, and it was dark and cold outside. I stood wondering which way to go. My stomach reminded me that it was time for supper. I had left the apartment so quickly that I hadn't taken any money with me. At least I had a handkerchief inside my pocket because I confess that I was crying tears of anger.

What could I do? I couldn't go to Mimi's. Her family has little enough for themselves. It would be terrible for them to have an uninvited guest for supper. Also Mimi shares her bed with two of her younger sisters. So not only would they not have food to spare, there would not be space for me to sleep. Then I remembered the public library. Some evenings it remains open until nine o'clock. At least I would be warm inside there, even if I couldn't fill my stomach and spend the whole night. I walked quickly, but imagine my annoyance when I arrived at the library and discovered that this was an evening when it closed at six.

I decided to keep walking. At least it kept me warm. I had so many angry words inside my head for Meyer that I was *talking* to him as I went up and down the streets. I must have walked for almost an hour when suddenly I felt a hand on my shoulder.

I let out a shriek of alarm.

"Dossi, it's Meyer," a voice called out as I started running.

It was a voice I recognized.

Considering that I had been talking with him in my head for almost sixty minutes, you'd think I'd have plenty to tell him about how I felt. But I was speechless. So it was up to Meyer to begin speaking.

"Are you crazy walking about at night?" he scolded me. "I've been looking all over for you. And Ruthi is home worrying herself sick."

"I'm sorry to upset Ruthi," I told him. "But you can't expect me to live with you any longer. You walk in the door and immediately begin yelling at me."

I had to stop to blow my nose. But I was determined not to let Meyer see me cry.

"I shouldn't have spoken to you as I did," Meyer said in a softer voice. "But I couldn't help it. I'm feeling very anxious these days. Ruthi is going to have a baby," he announced.

And then before I could even react to this piece of news, he gasped, "Oh, dear. Now I've said the wrong thing twice this evening. I promised Ruthi she could tell you. We were just waiting a few more days because we wanted to be sure everything was going well."

"And is she well?" I asked anxiously.

"Yes. She seems fine. But she tires easily just now, and that's what made me get so upset when I saw her standing at the stove and you sitting down. I couldn't help myself."

That was as close as Meyer came to apologizing to me. But I was too concerned about my sister to think about that just then.

"I'd much rather cook supper than do algebra," I told him.

"Algebra. That's easy," said Meyer.

"Easy for you, not easy for me," I said.

"How about letting me help you after supper?" he offered.

"If I'd known about the baby, I would have helped Ruthi more," I said. "Should I pretend not to know about it?"

"No. We must tell Ruthi the truth. She wanted to tell you as soon as she told me. But, but . . ."

I'd not forgotten that Meyer's first wife died during childbirth with a stillborn infant. So I realized that Ruthi's pregnancy was a bittersweet event for her husband. They wanted children, but he was worried about Ruthi's well being. I looked at his dimpled chin. It only affects the first wife, I told myself. It's only a superstition anyhow.

We went back home and ate an overcooked meal. But there was much hugging and tears between Ruthi and me. The baby is due in early July.

It's extraordinary news and a very happy ending to the fight that I had with Meyer. I wanted to tell you the happy news at once, and since you've become my confidante I had to tell you the full story: angry words, tears, and all. The big question now is will I have a niece or a nephew?

Your friend, soon to be an aunt,

Dossi

P.S. Meyer did such a good job helping me with my algebra that I got 100 percent on the examination we had in school today.

January 19, 1911

Dear Emma,

There has been only one small outburst between my brother-in-law and me since my last letter.

But regarding our health, I'm happy to report that Ruthi, Meyer, and I are all fine. Meyer takes credit for my physical well being because he urged Ruthi to send me to the country last summer. "I knew what Dossi needed was some good fresh air," he says. And perhaps he's right. This is the first winter that I haven't had bad colds and coughing attacks. All I've had was a case of sniffles that lasted just a few days. But I'm sure the better diet that Ruthi and I can have because of Meyer's good salary must affect my health. We eat many things now that I only admired before in the pushcarts. One does not get healthy *looking* at oranges and bananas. We also eat meat or fish several times a week. As a result, my clothing is getting tight on me. I'll need a new wardrobe soon.

But now that winter is really upon us, there is much sickness in the city. Meyer says it doesn't help matters that people carry their soiled handkerchiefs with them and reuse them over and over, spreading their germs around. He says it would be much better if a handkerchief was thrown into the trash once it was used. "Why are we saving those snot-filled rags?" he asked Ruthi when he saw her reusing one of her handkerchiefs.

"You make a fine living," she told him, keeping her good humor and not getting annoyed at his words. "But it's not so excessive that we can discard all our handkerchiefs. Besides, think of all the wasted labor. It takes me half an hour to neatly hem a square of cotton."

Imagine: Meyer predicts that in the future people will no longer reuse their handkerchiefs. "How will people be able to afford new handkerchiefs every time they sneeze?" I asked him. He doesn't know. But still he is certain that he is right. How silly he can be sometimes.

Here in our tenement building, Becky and Bluma, the two little girls who live beneath us, both had bad colds. Last Saturday I was going to take them outside and teach them how to jump rope with a piece of old clothesline that I had found. But they were coughing so badly that it seemed wiser to stay indoors playing quietly.

"Please, can we play with Sadie?" Bluma begged me. And she looked so pathetic, with her dripping nose and red-rimmed eyes, that I broke my rule and ran upstairs and brought my old rag doll down to my neighbors' apartment. Bluma smiled so happily, between coughing fits, that I even agreed to let my doll sleep in Bluma and Becky's bed overnight. "But tomorrow she must come home to where she lives," I said. It was as if I were talking about a real live child and not a toy. The next day, when Bluma had a fever and was feeling so much worse, I agreed to let Sadie remain a few more days to cheer her up.

At school there is much illness and absence, too. Not only do my classmates cough and blow their noses constantly, but even my teacher was forced to stay home from school for two days last week. The big problem is that there is fear of an epidemic.

Meyer knew about it first. Getting the prescriptions from the doctors gives him firsthand knowledge of what ailments are attacking the city residents. Unfortunately, even without Meyer's report, I would have discovered the news early, too. It turns out that both Becky and Bluma have been stricken.

At first we thought they just had the grippe. But hearing their coughs as he climbed the stairs to our apartment, Meyer forbid me to go near them.

"I promised their mother that I would entertain them while she went to deliver the collars that she has been working on," I told Meyer angrily. (Their widowed mother supports herself and her daughters by doing sewing work at home and taking in boarders.) How dare he forbid me to do anything, I thought.

"Dossi," he said. "This is very, very serious. I am certain that the girls have more than simple winter colds. And I don't want you to catch anything from them."

"That's a risk I'm willing to take," I retorted.

"But it's not a risk I am willing to take," he said sternly. "If you catch something, you may very likely pass it on to Ruthi. I don't want anything to happen to her."

And suddenly I felt very selfish. I had indeed wanted to play with Becky and Bluma, but I also wanted very much to establish my right to do as I please. Yet at once I realized what was behind my brother-in-law's warning to keep away from my little neighbors. Of course I don't want Ruthi to get ill, either.

So I stayed upstairs in our apartment cutting out paper dolls and drawing funny faces on them. I have some old Crayola crayons, and I used them to color in fancy dresses on the dolls. When I had made quite a supply, enough to entertain the children for many hours, I went downstairs and slid the dolls under their doorway.

An hour later, returning from the library with a new supply of books, I made a discovery. During the time that I was out of the building, a sign had been attached to the door of the Edelmans' apartment. There was only one word on it, but it gave me chills. *Quarantine.* It means that no one can enter or leave that apartment until the paper is removed. A quarantine sign is put up only when there is a very serious and contagious disease. Becky and Bluma have diphtheria.

As you know, diphtheria is a terrible illness that affects the breathing and is often fatal. Here in New York City, every year hundreds of people die from it. And most of the victims are children. Now I have so many worries. Are Becky and Bluma strong enough to recover from this awful sickness? And is it possible that I will come down with diphtheria, too? And will Ruthi get it next? It is too awful to think of all these things. So I will read my library books and escape into a fictional world.

I hope my next letter will bring better news.

Your friend,
Dossi

January 23, 1911

Dear Emma,

The quarantine sign is still on the door of the apartment below us. Everyone walking past can hear the sound of the two sisters coughing.

When the boarders arrived home from work last week and saw the sign, they were forced to look elsewhere for a place to sleep. This means that the girls' mother has temporarily lost a source of her income. She can't work, either, because the collars she would make cannot be delivered because, due to the quarantine, she should not leave the apartment. Meyer, who was so harsh when I wanted to go and help, has shown the softer side to his nature. He slid an envelope under the door with money inside. (My brother-in-law is like two people: one is caring and thoughtful, and the other is busy bossing me around.) Ruthi prepared a pot of stewed chicken and vegetables, which I carried downstairs and left by the Edelmans' door. It reminds me of *Little Women,* when Mrs. March and Beth go out to help people in their community. It seems so good and simple in the book, but of course, in real life, it represents a terrible time.

"We must pray for those two little girls," said Ruthi at supper last night. But the truth is, we're not very religious people, and I can't imagine why any God would listen to our requests when we don't do much to honor Him during good times.

Perhaps, however, you and Nell and your family, who attend church so regularly, will add a few words in your prayers for Becky and Bluma Edelman. I'm sure God would listen to you. And I'm certain that He cares for people regardless of their religion.

Your friend,
Dossi

Dear Emma,

You must wonder at the frequency of my letters these days. Do I seem very extravagant purchasing so many stamps and writing so often? It's because I have no one to speak freely to except you.

In the past, though we were poor and shared one bed, my life had a special pleasure. Ruthi and I would whisper in the dark before we fell asleep. Then I could tell her my thoughts and worries and she'd put her arm around me and calm me in her quiet, earnest way. Now I have my own private corner with my own bed. I'm lucky to have this, but I miss the chance to confide. Of course, I can talk to Ruthi during the day, but there are some things that are easier to speak of in the dark.

My other confidante has always been Mimi. However, these days she rushes home from school as soon as we are released. She must help her mother, and she has no time for conversations and walks with me. I realize this and I admire her. But I miss her, too. Luckily I have you! You are far away; still, I hope my letters make my troubles clear enough so you can understand. Becky and Bluma remain ill.

Today when I came home from school, the weather was a bit milder than it has been in recent days. We are getting closer to spring, I reminded myself. There is less illness in the good weather. Perhaps all will yet be well with my little friends, I thought.

Although there are thousands and thousands of people living in my neighborhood, after just a few months of living on this street, I can already recognize most of them by sight. I know which children live here, and I can match the children with their parents and pair the wives and husbands together, too. So yesterday when I came home from school and saw a dark-haired older woman sitting on the stoop (that's the stone step that leads up to the door of our tenement building), I knew at once she had a face I hadn't seen before. Then I noticed her dark blue outfit and hat and realized that she was one of a group of trained women who call on the sick as visiting nurses.

"Did you go to the Edelman apartment?" I asked her immediately. No one can enter or leave the apartment when the quarantine sign is there. But of course, an exception is made for doctors or nurses.

She nodded and took a bite of the apple that was in her hand.

"How are Becky and Bluma?" I asked anxiously.

"It's still too soon to tell," the woman said. "But their mother is keeping them clean and comfortable, which is good. People don't seem to realize how important cleanliness is in disease control."

"It's not easy to keep clean when all you have is a bit of cold water and no soap," I retorted, defending my neighbors. Ruthi always managed to find the coins to buy us soap, even when we had hardly any money; but when the choice is between soap and supper, everyone would select the latter.

The nurse opened the black satchel that was resting by her feet and showed me that she had a dozen bars of soap inside. "I give these away," she said, sighing. "But it's impossible for me to carry hot water."

"What else is in your bag?" I asked her curiously.

"Bandages, a thermometer, antiseptics, alcohol, ointments. Whatever might be useful. I'm not a doctor, but I do what I can to help."

"You do good work," I told her, regretting my sharp tone of a moment before. "A visiting nurse came several times when my mother was dying."

"I notice you say *dying*, so I guess the nurse couldn't help save your mother," the woman said.

"No. She had tuberculosis. It just got worse and worse," I said, blinking back tears. "My father died of it, too," I added.

"Was he a garment worker?" she asked me.

"Yes. A presser."

"We call tuberculosis the tailor's disease," the woman said, sighing. "So many of the workers succumb to it. There's not much we nurses can do to prevent the disease or to cure it when people are forced to work under bad conditions. But we keep on trying."

She reached into her bag and offered me an apple from inside.

"Isn't this your lunch?" I asked her.

"It's yesterday's lunch," she said, smiling. "I was too busy to eat it. And tomorrow's lunch is waiting in a bowl in my kitchen."

I took a bite of the apple, "Do you believe the saying An apple a day keeps the doctor away?" I asked.

"Cleanliness and good food are the two most important things to prevent disease. With more of both, doctors could sleep later and take more vacations."

"Well, at least you're bringing soap," I reminded her.

"Unfortunately, some people hide the soap away to save it for an important occasion. I try and impress them with the fact that soap is important every day, not just on the sabbath."

"They're afraid that there won't be any left for the sabbath," I pointed out.

"I understand that. But if they don't take care of themselves today, they may not live till the sabbath," she said.

The woman stood up and brushed off her skirt. "Perhaps when you're older, you'll study nursing and then join our visiting nurse service," she said to me.

"We'll never have all the workers we need for our job."

"Perhaps," I said. And then I asked her something that I've never discussed with Ruthi or Mimi or you.

"Do you think it's possible for a woman to become a doctor?" I asked.

"A doctor. Brava for such a wonderful thought!" she exclaimed. "I once thought of being a doctor myself, but I was too impatient to begin helping others, and it was much more difficult for a woman to become a doctor back in those days. So I dropped out of medical school and here I am.

"Now it's easier. There are colleges here in the city that give the science courses to prepare women for medical studies."

Then she held out her hand. "My name is Lillian Wald. I should have introduced myself before. I don't do as many home visits these days as I did in the past. But several of our nurses are ill themselves and we're short staffed today," she said. Then she smiled at me and added, "It has been a pleasure talking to you. Hold on to your goals." She thought a moment. "I don't believe you told me your name, either."

"I'm Hadassah Rabinowitz," I told her. "Everyone calls me Dossi."

"Good luck, Dossi," Miss Wald said as she picked up her bag and started down the street.

It was only after she had gone and I was discarding the damp apple core into a pail of trash in our kitchen that I recognized the woman's name. She is the founder of the visiting nurse service here in the city and a saint of saints, according to many. Her family has loads of money, and she could have spent her time traveling or sitting home painting watercolors and drinking tea from fancy china dishes. Instead, she has chosen to spend her days working hard to help others. In fact, she even lives in this area among the poor people she visits instead of in uptown Manhattan, where she could have a fine apartment. She insists that all the nurses who work under her live here, too.

When I mentioned to Ruthi and Meyer that I had met Lillian Wald, they could not say enough good things about her. "It was she who founded the Henry Street Settlement House," Meyer said, referring to a nearby organization that has programs to help new immigrants. He said Miss Wald was responsible for there being nurses in all the public schools in the city these days.

"Miss Wald petitioned the Metropolitan Museum

of Art to remain open on Sundays because that's the one day when workers might be free to take advantage of its exhibitions," Ruthi reminded me.

What an amazing woman that Miss Wald is. She gave me an apple, but she also gave me something more—the encouragement to aim for such an exalted profession. Wouldn't it be amazing? Wouldn't it be wonderful if someday I am,

Your friend,

Dr. Hadassah Rabinowitz

February 10, 1911

Dear Emma,

What grand news your last letter brought. Congratulations to your brother Eddie on his betrothal to Libby Greene. I didn't get to meet her during my visit to your home last summer, but I certainly heard her name mentioned more than once. You say he will be married in May. That is a lovely month to hold a wedding. I will want to hear every detail from you about the event. Where will Eddie and Libby live? If not with you, will your father be able to manage the farm work with just your brother Timothy helping him? Will you have to help him milk the cows?

Here we have good news, too. Both Becky and Bluma have completely recovered from diphtheria. I discovered that the quarantine sign was down from their apartment when I returned home from school one day last week. I stopped at once and knocked on their door. The girls, looking pale and smaller than ever, stood behind their mother when she opened the door.

"Oh, I am so happy!" I shouted when I caught sight of them. I dropped my books and ran to hug both girls.

Bluma began bawling loudly. "What is it? Do you still feel ill?" I asked, puzzled by her behavior.

"Something terrible happened," Bluma cried.

"It's not our fault," Becky added. She, too, was crying.

I looked at their mother. "I don't understand," I said. "The quarantine sign is down. The girls aren't coughing. What is the matter?"

"They're afraid you'll be angry with them about the burning," she said.

"What are you talking about?" I asked.

"When a quarantine is lifted, all the household items that were handled by the ill, like the bedclothes and storybooks and toys, are burned to destroy the germs."

"I know. I've seen it done," I replied.

"But they burned Sadie. I didn't want them to, but they took her away," sobbed Bluma.

"Sadie? *My* Sadie."

"They burned our paper dolls, too," added Becky. As if I'd care about those little pieces of paper that I'd cut and colored for them.

Oh, Emma, I am so ashamed of myself. But I began crying, too. The thought of my one special possession stitched by hand by my mother having been destroyed was more than I could bear. I turned and raced up the stairs.

Ruthi was waiting for me. "Wasn't that a wonderful surprise?" she asked before she saw my tears. She'd thought I'd be so delighted to see Becky and Bluma well again. And so I had been until I realized the fate of my old Sadie. "They burned my doll. They burned my doll," I said over and over again.

"It was only a toy," Ruthi said when she understood why I was crying. "How can you care about that dirty old thing? You should be ashamed of yourself, acting like a baby. This is a moment of rejoicing.

Becky and Bluma could have died."

Oh, Emma. Nothing Ruthi said could stop my tears. I lay on my bed and cried for a long, long time. I must have fallen asleep because the next thing I knew it was dark outside. I could hear Meyer's voice coming from the table, so I knew his workday was over and he and my sister must have been eating. I didn't get up. I didn't want to see him or Ruthi. I just lay on my bed, facing the wall, and felt sorry for myself. I remembered that, as recently as a few months ago, I would take Sadie into bed with me. Now I would never be able to stroke her red yarn hair or admire the tiny stitches that my mother had made when she sewed her body together. Even her old dress was a precious memory because it was made out of the same fabric as a dress that my mother once wore. I kept imagining Sadie in the midst of flames, burning bit by bit until she was reduced to nothing more than ashes.

After a long while, I heard footsteps approaching my bed. "Dossi, are you awake?" Ruthi called softly, and she pulled the curtain aside.

"Yes," I whispered back.

She came and sat on my bed. "Dossi," she said. "Mama would be pleased that you loved that old rag doll so well. But she wouldn't want you to mourn her. Besides, I'm sure that if Mama was still alive, you wouldn't have kept the doll all this time. You would have given her away or even thrown her on a garbage heap. You're almost ready to graduate from elementary school. In a few months you'll be enrolled in high school. High school girls don't play with dolls. You didn't play with that old doll anymore yourself. She just sat on your chest gathering dust."

"That's not true," I said, sitting up in bed. "I didn't play with Sadie like I once did. But she never gathered dust. I touched her and thought of Mama many times every week. She was the one thing I had that Mama had touched, too."

Ruthi put her arms around me. "Dossi," she said. "You forget that Mama touched you and she touched me. And we're still here. When the baby is born, if we have a girl, she will be given Mama's name."

"That's good," I said, sniffing back new tears.

"Here," Ruthi said, taking my hand and putting something in it. Even though it was dark in the room, I could feel what she'd given me.

"I kept this for a time. But now I want you to have it," Ruthi said.

She was giving me the brooch that had belonged to our mother.

"But it's yours. She gave it to you because you're the oldest," I said, stroking the pin. I could remember stroking it when it was attached to my mother's good black dress. It's a cameo of a woman. When I was little, I always thought the woman was actually Mama. Only when I got older did I realize it wasn't her silhouette.

"Papa gave this brooch to Mama. Mama gave it to me. And now I'm giving it to you," Ruthi said. "Someday you'll give it to someone, too. Perhaps you'll give it to your daughter."

"Suppose I don't have a daughter?" I asked her.

"Then you will have to give it to mine," she replied.

And then we both laughed. It was funny to be discussing children who didn't even exist and perhaps never will. After all, Ruthi may become the mother of many sons.

"Thank you," I said, kissing Ruthi. "You're such a good sister to me. And I'll let you borrow this back whenever you want to. It looks so fine on your brown dress when you go out with Meyer."

"Yes," Ruthi agreed. "It does look well on my

dress. But you know, next week is my birthday, and I have a feeling that Meyer is planning to give me a brooch of my own—just the way Papa once gave this one to Mama."

So that, dear Emma, is the latest news I have to report. Good news and bad. But really, the bad news wasn't so very terrible once I recovered from my childish sorrow. And if you lived nearby, I would gladly lend you my brooch to wear on your dress at Eddie's wedding.

Your friend,
Dossi

February 20, 1911

Dear Nell,

I just heard that you broke your ankle while ice skating. It must be awful not to be able to walk and play. I hope Emma is bringing you many good books from the library and I hope that you will be better soon and be able to walk down the aisle as the flower girl at your brother's wedding.

Love,
Dossi

February 23, 1911

Dear Emma,

When I went to the post office a couple of days ago to buy the stamps that I put on my card to Nell and the letter to you, the clerk behind the counter said to me, "Are you here again? I think you eat the stamps I sell you. I believe you mistake them for candies."

I didn't know how to respond. Since then I've been thinking about what I should have said: *Yes, their flavor is delightful.* Or *No, they do not sit well with my digestion.* Well, I bought half a dozen stamps that day, so I'll have a bit more time to consider my comment if he jokes with me again.

I was very sorry to learn about Nell's accident. I have never done any ice skating myself, but a few times I've watched others. There's a lake in Central Park that freezes over and many people go there to skate. I've heard that when the park first opened there was a "skating mania," and sometimes as many as thirty thousand people came in a single day to skate or watch others. The number sounds absurd. How could one see anything with so many people blocking the view? And what lake is large enough for so many people to skate at one time? Still, that is what I've read in the paper. And for you, in your country locale, the number thirty thousand must seem not only absurd, but impossible. Anyhow, I hope that poor Nell recovers quickly. It must be awkward to be helpless without assistance for even the most intimate needs. And remembering Nell's lively and outgoing personality, I am sure she will hate staying home from school and not being with other people until she can manage without aid. But I know your family will help her through this unpleasant time.

The other item that you wrote about in your last letter I haven't yet mentioned. It's the invitation to return to Jericho this coming summer. I'm delighted to be asked, even though the summer still seems so far in the future. You know how much I enjoyed my time with you. And if things were the same as a year ago, I should immediately say YES. But since Ruthi is expecting the baby in July, I feel I must wait and see what her needs are. Perhaps she will be weak or tired after the birth. Perhaps the baby will be colicky and keep her awake all night. I must be here to offer my help. Ever since the big scene I had with Meyer, I am very conscious about being helpful. But I do it because I love her, not because Meyer said I must. In any event, I hope you can be patient about waiting for an answer from me about the summer. However, if you must make a decision now about whether to invite another Fresh Air child in my place, I will understand. Perhaps it is greedy of me to even consider repeating my wonderful holiday when there are other children who haven't yet experienced the joys and surprises of a visit in the country.

Since my last letter, Ruthi celebrated her birthday. She was nineteen years old on February 21st. I came home from school and baked a cake for the occasion. It was a simple one-egg cake, but I made some sugar icing to put on top (which was good because it hid the part of the cake that was slightly burnt). The day before, I had gone to the Triangle Shirtwaist

Factory at closing time and waited until I saw Rosa Capaccio leaving work. Even though I'd been there before, I was amazed anew at the number of girls and women who left the factory at five o'clock when the work day ended. It seemed impossible that so many people, at least five hundred, Ruthi has said, could fit inside one building. Finally I spotted Rosa. "Can you come and have supper with us tomorrow?" I asked her. "We'll celebrate Ruthi's and your birthdays together."

Rosa must have been very tired after her long day. She has to arrive by a quarter to seven each morning. But her face lit up at my news. "What a wonderful plan," she exclaimed, hugging me. "Of course I will come," she promised.

So on the evening of the 21st, there were four of us sitting around the supper table—four and a half if you count the unborn child growing inside Ruthi. For a gift I gave my sister several colored ribbons that I had bought off a pushcart on nearby Orchard Street. Ruthi has a way of weaving a ribbon through her hair that makes her look very regal. Rosa gave her an artificial flower, a rose, of course, also to be worn in her hair. Rosa's sister-in-law makes the flowers at home and sells them to a milliner who sews them onto hats.

Ruthi had a gift for Rosa, too: a bottle of toilet water that she bought at Meyer's pharmacy. *Toilet water* is a very funny name for perfume. This one smelled like roses. Very appropriate! Rosa flushed with pleasure.

From Meyer, Ruthi received a brooch, just as she had predicted. It is made of silver, and in the center there is a lovely stone of a beautiful blue-green color. "It's a turquoise," Meyer explained. The piece of jewelry was made by Indians from the Southwest. It's a beautiful pin, but I shall always love my brooch, which came from Mama, the best.

I examined Ruthi's pin with interest. We studied about the Indians at school a few years back, but I never expected to touch something that an Indian had made. Ruthi immediately went to the mirror in her bedroom and twisted a ribbon in her hair and added her new flower. She attached the brooch to her dress. "I think I am ready to go to the opera," she joked when she returned to the table, tossing her head and looking very elegant.

"Then we'll have to serenade you ourselves, since I don't have any opera tickets," Meyer said. And believe it or not, we all sang together just as you and your family do when you visit with your neighbor Mr. Bentley at his home. We didn't have his piano accompaniment, but Meyer has a strong voice and so he carried us along as we sang some popular songs like "Down by the Old Mill Stream" and "Meet Me in St. Louis."

While we were singing, I had only the pleasantest thoughts about Meyer. It is very evident that he has made Ruthi very happy. It's not his fault that he's forced to have his young sister-in-law living in a corner of his apartment. I guess he wishes for privacy from me just as much as I wish for some privacy away from him.

Everyone admired my cake despite the burnt corner. (I carefully cut and ate that portion myself.) Rosa entertained us with stories about the workers at the factory, gossip about who was fighting with whom and who was hoping to get married shortly.

"Annie Giamatti lost a tooth while she was sewing last week," Rosa reported. "She stuck the tooth into the pocket of the shirt she was working on and said, 'Whoever buys this will get more than they expect for their money.'" Rosa laughed heartily as she told us this story.

Despite her long hours at work, she seemed merry

and energetic. When she laughs, it makes you want to laugh, too. "Infectious," Meyer said later. But infectious in a good sense, not like diphtheria!

"We must save our money and buy you some gold teeth to replace those that you are missing," Meyer said to Rosa at one point.

I turned at once to look at Rosa. I was certain that she would take offense that he mentioned the spaces in her mouth. But Rosa has a wonderful sense of humor. Instead of getting annoyed at my brother-in-law, she laughed and laughed. "Yes, yes," she agreed with him. "With a pair of shiny gold teeth, I would be sure to catch a rich husband. And if my husband ever lost his money, we could pawn my teeth to tide us over until good times returned."

Meyer and Ruthi laughed with Rosa. But I felt a little sad. So many people in our area regularly pawn their possessions to get a little cash. That means they sell them to a dealer. When they have a bit of money in their pocket again, they can buy back their former possessions. It is a sad cycle. I remember my father had a gold watch that Mama pawned and redeemed several times until finally the time came when she didn't have any money to buy the watch back again. The owner of the pawn shop then sold it to someone else. Now somewhere in New York City there is a man carrying my papa's watch that was given to him by his papa—a watch that traveled across the Atlantic Ocean and one that no one in my family will ever see again. Does he pretend the *R* engraved on its back stands for Ruben or Roberts or some other name? He'll never know that the initial stands for Rabinowitz.

"What are you thinking about, Dossi?" Rosa asked, poking me. "You look so serious."

I remembered it was a birthday party and quickly tried to clear my thoughts and suggested that we sing another song. We sang "Daisy, Daisy," and Meyer helped Ruthi up from her chair and began to dance around the table with her. Ruthi no longer wears the belts on any of her dresses, and so they hang loose. But anyone who knows her, and even those who don't, recognizes that the girth beneath the fabric is the child inside her.

When it was time for Rosa to leave, she hugged Ruthi tightly. "I think about you even if we don't see each other often," she told my sister. "I'm going to make an outfit for your baby," she said, rubbing her hand along Ruthi's stomach.

"And I think of you, sweet Rosa," Ruthi said with

tears in her eyes as she returned the hug. I know she wishes her friend could have the good fortune to marry and have her own family, too. "We'll plan to see you again soon," Ruthi promised. "In the spring we will make a picnic in the park."

"Yes, yes," Rosa said. "I love picnics. But Dossi must promise to bake us another cake. Just like the one we had this evening."

"Another burnt cake?" I asked. "You shall have it."

Meyer escorted Rosa back home. We think our neighborhood is safe, but from time to time one hears of thieves or drunkards who disturb people. It was one of the reasons that Ruthi was so worried about me the evening I ran off. With Meyer at her side, Rosa would not have to worry.

I told Ruthi to sit still and I cleared away and washed all the dishes. I cut the remaining piece of cake in half. One half to be shared by Ruthi and Meyer tomorrow and the other half for Bluma and Becky. I think they'll like my cake even more than the paper dolls I make for them.

Love,
Dossi

March 15, 1911

Dear Emma,

I was so happy to get your most recent letter yesterday and to read the words, "We will wait for you to make a decision about the summer, and we're all hoping that it will be to come for another visit."

It is what I'm hoping for, too, but it's much too soon to know what the future will bring. And should your family change its mind and decide to invite another child to be the summer visitor, I promise I will understand.

Here I am unsure of my summer plans, but during the past couple of days all we've talked about at school is next autumn: Who is continuing on beyond eighth grade? Who is applying for working papers? Who will go to night classes and who will study during the day? Which school do friends want to attend?

I filled out all the forms that were distributed. I marked that I had an interest in science, but I didn't dare to reveal more. Perhaps I'll do poorly, and my dream of becoming a doctor will remain only a dream.

The school where I plan to enroll is named Washington Irving High School. I can walk there from our tenement in about twenty minutes (longer if I am carrying a heavy load of school books). I'm sure you've heard that name before. He was an early nineteenth-century writer, most famous for the story *Rip Van Winkle* and also *The Legend of Sleepy Hollow*. I'd already read both of those books, but now that I know I shall be attending a school that is named in his honor, I went to the library and checked those titles out to reread them.

Meanwhile Ruthi is beaming proudly. She didn't study beyond the eighth grade, and though she always insisted that was enough book learning for her, she is delighted that I will have the chance to continue. "Mama and Papa would be so happy," she says. Papa was a great scholar and loved reading, although in his last years he was too tired when he returned home from work to do more than read an occasional newspaper. But I have a childhood memory of him poring over a heavy book. It was before he left for America and when we were still living in our old home in Russia. I wonder what the book was. I think it must have been a Bible or a prayer book.

As for Meyer, he nods at me and says, "Don't forget. If it wasn't for my help with your arithmetic, you might have to repeat eighth grade next year." That made me angry. It's true that he helped me with my homework, but I would never have failed the subject. Perhaps he is jealous that one day he won't be the only one in this family to have a college degree. He studied pharmacy at Columbia College.

Mimi is not going to high school. I feel very sad because I will miss her. These days I see so little of her. We eat our lunch together at school, but we never do our homework together as we did in the past. She always has to rush home to help her mother with the younger children in their family. Next year she'll be a wage earner when she begins to work in one of the clothing factories. I wish I could find a pot of gold, and not just a small hoard of coins as I did

when I removed the linoleum from my floor. Then
I would help everyone I know who needs money.
What a fantasy! I guess I've been reading too many
fairy tales.

Your friend,
Dossi

March 26, 1911

Dear Emma,

I have the most tragic news to report. But perhaps you have already heard about it. It is the only thing people here are talking about, and it's the headline in every newspaper in the city. So I would not be surprised to learn it was reported in the Vermont newspapers, too.

Yesterday in the late afternoon, there was a big fire at the Triangle Shirtwaist Factory, the very place where Ruthi used to work and where Rosa is still employed. The factory is located on the top three floors of the ten-story Asch Building, not too far from here. How the fire began, no one is sure. Most

likely some careless person dropped a burning cigarette. Because there were so many scraps of fabric and
so much lint on the wooden floors, it quickly ignited
and a blaze developed instantly. Of course, it caused
panic. But when the workers, mostly young girls
and women, ran to the doors to escape, they were
locked in.

Can you believe such a horror? The factory owners
regularly locked the doors so that no one could leave
work early or perhaps steal a garment. The women
ran to the windows, but they were so high above the
street level that at first no one dared to jump.

Of course, the fire engines came. But the ladders
that they raised were not tall enough to reach the
workers. There was chaos. Screaming and yelling. The
firemen urged the women to jump from the windows into nets that they held out. Imagine what a
terrifying thing that was to do, but some women
bravely held hands with their coworkers and jumped.
And then came still another part of this tragedy. The
strong force of their falling bodies pulled the nets out
of the firemen's hands, and so the women crashed
directly on the ground. Dead. Others died jumping
from windows as the flames reached their clothes.

Emma, they are still counting the dead bodies.

Every available ambulance in all of Manhattan came to take those bodies to the morgue. They haven't made a full count yet, but already they know that over a hundred women have died in this tragedy.

When I heard the dreadful sound of the fire engines racing to the fire, I ran out from the public library where I had gone to borrow books. I heard someone say that it was the Asch Building that was burning, and I immediately thought of Rosa. Was she safe? I wanted to see what was happening for myself, not because I wanted to view such a morbid tragedy, but because I just couldn't believe the news. Hadn't my own sister been working there only a few months ago? When I reached Greene Street, near the site of the factory, I could smell the smoke. But I couldn't see a thing. There were so many fire engines and ambulances, policemen and gawkers. The word had spread quickly, and family members came looking for their relatives who were employed at the factory. Strangers stood talking to one another in Yiddish and Russian, Italian, and broken English, and with all those accents. Men and women stood weeping. It was a terrible sight to see so many people crying, I couldn't even see the factory where the real horror had occurred. I stood there shaking with emotion. My teeth began chattering, and I couldn't control them. Oh Rosa, I thought. Please, please be safe.

Loud screams filled the air. I didn't know if they were the voices of still more victims falling to their deaths or of the people on the street who were viewing this scene and perhaps recognizing a dead family member.

I kept thinking about how good it was that Ruthi didn't work there any longer. Meyer had predicted that something like this could happen. What if Ruthi hadn't met Meyer? What if Meyer hadn't insisted that she stop working? What if she hadn't agreed with him and had continued working, at least until the baby was born? There were so many possibilities and one seemed worse than another. I pushed my way out of the crowd and made my way home.

Ruthi was waiting. "What's happening?" she asked, not knowing the extent of the fire but having already heard rumors about it from our neighbors.

I began explaining what I knew, which at that point was still limited. I didn't know that so many were dead. That it was a miracle if anyone survived at all.

"And Rosa? Did you see Rosa?" my sister asked.

"No," I admitted. "There were so many people and so much smoke, it was hard to make out faces. But maybe she escaped," I said with more hope than I felt. "They said some workers were saved. I heard that several women climbed up to the roof, and students from New York University helped them as they jumped across the roof to the next building." I wondered if Rosa would have thought to do that. If she made it to the tenth floor, this was a possibility. But if she was on the eighth floor, the flames would have engulfed her before she could reach the roof. I wanted to ask Ruthi to remind me on which floor she had worked. But I couldn't. I didn't want to hear her answer.

Ruthi and I held each other and wept. We wept for the women Ruthi had worked with, women she had laughed with and women with whom she sometimes had angry words. We wept for Rosa, though we didn't know her fate. We cried and cried.

When Meyer came home, his pale face showed he, too, knew what had occurred.

He took one look at us and turned and ran back down the stairs. "Where is he going?" Ruthi asked me.

I didn't know. But when he returned a short while later, I realized that he had gone back to the pharmacy where he works. He brought some powders, which he mixed in water, and insisted that Ruthi and I drink at once. I don't know what it was. I don't remember what it tasted like. But I realize now it was something to calm us. After a while Ruthi and I lay down on our beds and slept. But when we woke, we both remembered again what had taken place.

This morning I've been sitting with Ruthi and trying to distract her and keep her calm. She told me that there were several small fires when she worked at the factory, but that they had always managed to extinguish them quickly. "Why didn't you tell me that before?" I demanded to know.

"What was the point?" Ruthi said, weeping. "You would just have worried every day when I went off to work."

Of course she is right. And I can only be relieved that at least she confided such information to Meyer when they were courting. No wonder he was so adamant about her leaving the factory. Of course, Meyer is worried that all this upset is not good for Ruthi and the baby. Just now my sister is napping.

I will write again when I learn more. We're hoping that we will find out good news about Rosa before the day is over. Pray for her.

Your friend,
Dossi

Dear Emma,

Rosa is dead.

Yesterday, which was Monday, instead of going to school, I went with Ruthi to Rosa's home. As we walked along the street, we saw many people standing about and speaking. Everyone was still talking about the fire. There doesn't seem to be a person around here who didn't lose a relative, a friend, or an acquaintance in that terrible fire. And, because so many people in this area work in the garment industry, in places not unlike the Triangle Shirtwaist Factory, everyone shudders, knowing that this tragedy could so easily have happened to them or their relatives.

When we reached Rosa's tenement, we were afraid to go in. As long as we stood outside, we could pretend that Ruthi's friend was saved. But the moment we entered, we would know the truth. And indeed, we both knew it before we were told. Rosa was dead. There were her red-eyed brother and sister-in-law planning the funeral service while her little nieces and nephew chased one another around the room. They're too young to understand what has happened. And the fact is, even grown people like Ruthi and me can't quite understand it, either. How could such a disaster occur? As for Rosa, no one is certain if she jumped or was pushed from one of the windows. Does it matter? She is gone.

Ruthi sat in Rosa's family's crowded rooms and sobbed again. "We needed her earnings," Rosa's sister-in-law said over and over again. I wondered if she was annoyed that the family has lost part of its income or if she was trying to explain why Rosa had been forced to work at the factory.

When we learned where and when the funeral would take place, Ruthi and I promised we would return. Then I helped Ruthi up and started back home with her. She leaned on me in a way that she had never done before. I kept trying to think of things to distract her, but everything I started to say and everything I saw reminded me of Rosa. The gold teeth she will never get, the husband she will never find, the picnic we will never have, Ruthi's baby that she will never hold, and the baby outfit she will never sew.

I thought about the fire and how terrifying it must have been for her. I hope she died quickly and without pain. And then suddenly, thinking of the flames that burned through those floors of the factory, I was reminded of that much, much smaller fire that had been set to burn Becky and Bluma's bedclothes and books and my doll. How silly it seemed now that I had cried for a toy. What pain could an old rag doll feel? No wonder Ruthi had called me a child. Belatedly, I was very ashamed of my tears.

All these thoughts about fire also made me recall the night last summer when your neighbors', the Turners, barn burned to the ground. We worried about the animals and about the men who had gone inside to rescue them. Miraculously, no one was hurt last summer. But it made me think. Our worlds are so different, you living out in the country surrounded by farmland and animals, and I here in a very crowded city with tenement buildings right on top of one another. Yet in both worlds, fire can and does cause terrible destruction and devastation. And that's also true about disease. People get sick in the country and the city. In both places people are born, grow, work, marry, bear children, and die. And it doesn't matter if one is Christian or Jew, white or of another race. Life is life. And death is the end for everyone. Does this sound simplistic? I just mean that whatever happens in your future or mine, there will be more similarities than differences.

Ruthi is so upset by the fire and Rosa's death that she has totally lost her appetite. She hasn't eaten anything in the past three days. "We knew the factory was dangerous. We knew the doors were locked," Ruthi says over and over again. "That's one of the things the girls were striking about last spring. Oh, why didn't Rosa and I join them? Why were we such cowards? If we'd been part of the strike, it might have made a difference."

"Two more girls would not have softened the hearts of the greedy factory owners," Meyer says, trying to calm my sister.

We're very worried about her. Meyer brought

home dried figs and dates that he purchased off one of the pushcarts. Ordinarily these dried fruits would be a big treat. He hoped that they would appeal to Ruthi's appetite. He was wrong.

I remembered how Ruthi had given me our mother's brooch to ease my sorrow at losing Sadie. But there's nothing I can offer my sister to console her on the loss of her friend. Nothing at all.

I spent three hours yesterday afternoon reading to Ruthi from one of my library books. I was hoping to distract her, but I don't think she heard a word. I'm not sure I understood what I read either. And in fact, if you ask me what book it was, I can't remember.

Now I notice that my tears have splashed on these pages, and the ink has smudged and blurred. I suppose I should copy this letter over again so that you can read it without difficulty, but I have no energy. You must read between the blurs or not at all. Forgive me for burdening you with all these sorrows. I have no one but you to share this with. You are far away, but when I write, I feel as if we're sitting side by side and I'm talking with you.

Your friend,
Dossi

Dear Emma,

These past days have been hard. In the streets people still talk about the Triangle fire. And at home Ruthi stays in her bed. She has no appetite and no energy. She cries constantly. I don't remember her crying as much when our mother died. I suppose then she felt she had to remain strong because she was responsible for me. Now these tears seem to be an accumulation for all the sorrows she has ever felt.

The baby is due in early July. If Ruthi doesn't eat, the baby can't grow. And worse, what is going to happen to Ruthi? Meyer's face is pinched and drawn these days, too. He looks at Ruthi and he, too, has no appetite. I've been coming home from school and cooking our supper. Roast chicken, fried fish, stewed fruit. Ruthi won't even taste the food. All she exists on these days is a little sweetened tea and perhaps a small piece of bread.

"Think of the baby," I whisper to her. "Try the fruit. I made it the way Mama used to."

"Mama is gone," Ruthi mumbles back to me. "Papa is gone. Velvel is gone." Our little brother Velvel died even before we came to America, when he was still a small child.

"But Ruthi, *we're* here," I remind her.

"Rosa is gone. Annie is gone. Clara is gone. Sylvia is gone." Ruthi goes on with her list, naming all of her former coworkers who died in the fire. Then she even adds the name of Meyer's deceased wife, whom she never knew.

"Ruthi. Just one spoonful," I say, treating her like a baby. I put a spoonful of the fruit to her mouth. If she said just one more name, I could slip the fruit inside her mouth when it was open. But Ruthi has run out of names. Or energy. She doesn't say anything more, and I put the spoon back in the dish.

I've been bringing some of the food I prepare downstairs to Becky and Bluma and their mother. At least someone should eat it. The little sisters are still pale from their illness. But it's already April. Soon it will be warm enough for them to play outside every day. The sun and air will be good for them, I think, and then I realize that I am beginning to sound like Meyer. As a pharmacist, it is strange that he thinks so highly about the sun and air instead of the tonics and powders that are sold in the shop where he works.

Today, hurrying home from school, I met Miss Wald again. She recognized me and smiled. "How are you, my dear?" she asked. And then she added, "Forgive me. I've forgotten your name."

"Dossi," I reminded her.

"Of course. I meet so many, many people each week that my brain can't hold them all," she said. And then she looked at me intently with her dark brown eyes and said, "Tell me. Did you lose anyone in the fire?"

I explained that no one in our family worked at the factory now, but that my sister, who used to work there, had lost her closest friend. "She suffers as if she was burned," I said. "She knew so many of the victims. Even people who she didn't like, the woman who stole her sewing needles and the woman who gossiped and said mean things about the others, perished, and she mourns for them, too."

"Give her time," Miss Wald said. "We can all still smell the stench from that fire in our nostrils. In time your sister's grief will abate. And I'll tell you something else," Miss Wald added. "Those girls who died have become martyrs to the labor cause. When they went out on strike for more wages and better conditions, no one paid attention to them. It's a terrible thing, and the truth is that I can name well over a hundred other loft areas that are even more at risk for a fire than the Triangle Factory. But the fire has brought the city's and the country's attention to the plight of those poor workers and the dangerous conditions. There will be changes ahead, I'm certain of that now. And there will be changes in your sister, too," she said, patting me on the shoulder.

"But we don't have much time," I said, and began explaining about the baby that was due in less than three months.

"You have a big job ahead of you, Dossi," Miss Wald said. "You must help your sister. Get her to eat. Cheer her up."

"But I've been trying," I said. "Nothing seems to work. I can't do it."

"That is the wrong attitude to take," Miss Wald said, putting her arm around me. "You know, when I began my work here, people said that nothing could help the people. 'They are dirty and ignorant,' I was told. But I knew they were tired and poor. There is still so much, much more to be done. But I'll never give up helping them. And you mustn't give up taking care of your sister."

I nodded. Of course I knew she was right. I couldn't give up helping Ruthi. I went home and made a pot of chicken soup. I even prepared some noodles to put in the broth. Ruthi ate only a few spoonfuls, but at least Meyer ate a full bowl.

"You are becoming a wonderful cook," he said approvingly. He turned to Ruthi. "She will make some man a fine wife one of these days."

Ruthi made a half smile at his joke.

After supper as I was cleaning up, Meyer opened his newspaper and read some of the more amusing articles aloud to Ruthi. She sat with her hands folded in her lap and appeared to be listening. But I knew she wasn't. Oh, Emma. I wish I knew how to get inside her head and clean out all the terrible thoughts the way I can sweep the dust from the corners of our rooms. Maybe then she would be able to eat again and the baby inside her could thrive.

Love,
Dossi

April 10, 1911

Dear Emma,

Several days ago as I left for school, I stopped to give some muffins that I had made to Bluma and Becky's mother. The two girls stood forlornly watching me. They're too young for school, and they can't go out on the street unsupervised. So they spend their hours inside bored and restless. Their mother keeps busy sewing collars and can't do more than serve them meals.

"Can't you stay and play with us?" Bluma begged me.

"I have to go to school," I reminded her. "Maybe when I come home this afternoon, I can play with you for a little while. It depends on whether my teacher gives me homework or not."

I knew that the afternoon must seem like a hundred years off in time to the two little girls.

"I wish Sadie didn't burn," Becky said. "Then we could play with her."

"Shhh," Mrs. Edelman said to them. She, like her daughters, is embarrassed about the loss of my doll.

"Don't worry about Sadie," I said. "There are many other dolls in the world."

I gave the girls quick hugs and started off to school. But an idea had just begun growing inside me. When I came home in the afternoon, I didn't stop to see the girls. Instead, I raced up the stairs to our apartment. There was Ruthi sitting on a chair, holding some knitting in her lap. But I could see that she had placed herself in that position and the knitting was just resting on her lap to convince me that she was doing something. It was a baby blanket that she had begun several weeks ago, and it was not one inch closer to completion than it had been before the fire.

I greeted my sister and she nodded automatically. I tried talking to her, but I could see she was hardly paying attention. However, I had a plan. I went to my corner and got my newest shirtwaist, which Ruthi had made for my birthday. It's a cream color with blue rickrack.

"Where are your scissors?" I asked Ruthi.

Of course I know where she keeps her scissors, but I wanted to be sure she knew that I was taking them. She looked at me without emotion and pointed to her sewing basket. I went and got the scissors. I laid my dress out on the table and pretended that I was going to cut into it.

As I hoped, this got her attention. "What are you doing?" she asked, puzzled.

"I want to make rag dolls for Bluma and Becky. They're downstairs all day long with nothing to do. They need something to play with. If I cut up my dress, I can use the fabric for the dolls' bodies. I want to make them dolls like my old Sadie. But these will be theirs to keep."

"You'll ruin your good dress," Ruthi said. I'm sure she was remembering all the hours of labor she had put into making it for me.

"I know. But I feel so bad for those two little girls. I'm going to sacrifice my dress to this cause."

"You sew even worse than you knit," Ruthi said. I

guess she was thinking of the dropped stitches in your holiday mittens.

"I'll do my best," I said, opening and closing the scissors. "Unless you want to help me."

"I'm not going to cut up your good dress," Ruthi said with more energy than she'd had in the past days.

I waited a moment as Ruthi got up and came over to the table. She picked up my shirtwaist dress and handed it to me. "Put this away," she said. "There's an old sheet that I could use instead of this." The next thing I knew, Ruthi pulled out the bureau drawer and was looking for the worn sheet.

Before long the table was covered with scraps of fabric, and Ruthi had cut out two rag dolls. "We'll stuff them with some of the leftover cloth," she said as she threaded a needle.

"Can you give the dolls dark brown hair?" I asked. "You have yarn that's just the right color from the muffler you made for Meyer."

I looked inside Ruthi's sewing box. It contains scraps from all the dresses and shirts that she's sewn in recent years. "Oh, look. These buttons would make perfect eyes," I said.

"No. They are too big. These are better," said

Ruthi, digging through the box and retrieving a handful of small blue buttons that had once been on a blouse of our mother's.

By the time Meyer came home from the drugstore, Ruthi had begun sewing the first doll. I told her that I had too much schoolwork to do that evening to help her, and she never thought to ask me how it was that just a short while before I was prepared to do all the sewing myself. This project had to be done by Ruthi, and although I was eager for the dolls to be completed, I knew it would be better if she couldn't finish them in one or two days. She needed more time with these rag dolls to break the spell that had drained her of interest in life.

Meyer looked at me with surprise when Ruthi helped herself to some of the potatoes and carrots that I cooked for supper. He told us an amusing story about a stray cat who had given birth to a litter of kittens in the basement of the building where the drugstore is located. "People don't have money to feed animals, but cats can find their own food," he said, referring to the mice and rats that run along the street at night.

"The baby kittens were as tiny as my finger," he said, holding up his hand.

Ruthi smiled. "I hope our baby is bigger than that," she said. It was the first positive mention of the baby in two weeks.

"Don't you think that shirt of yours is getting too worn?" Ruthi suddenly said to Meyer. He looked down at the striped shirt that he was wearing.

"Do you think so?" he asked, puzzled.

"The collar and cuffs are very frayed," Ruthi told her husband.

"Can't you turn them?" Meyer asked. That's what Ruthi usually does when shirts get old.

I knew what was in Ruthi's mind, however. "It doesn't pay," I told Meyer. "The shirt fabric is so faded. I don't think you should wear it to work again. It won't make a good impression on your customers."

"Really?" Meyer asked. "Should I take it off now?" he joked. "I don't want to make a poor impression on the two of you."

Of course he didn't take his shirt off as we sat at supper. But I knew that Ruthi had just gotten the material she needed for undergarments for the rag dolls.

Well, now the dolls are finished. They are darling, with blue button eyes and dark brown yarn hair. Ruthi braided the dolls' hair and cut up one of the ribbons I gave her for her birthday to tie at the ends. They each have a frock made of fabric scraps and trimmed with rickrack. "I'm beginning to wish that I was five years old," I told her.

This afternoon I went downstairs and invited Bluma and Becky to come up to our apartment. "There're some people I want you to meet," I told them.

The girls entered our apartment shyly. They didn't know who the people would be. When they saw the two dolls lying side by side on the table, their eyes widened with surprise.

"What are their names?" they asked. "Are they yours?"

"I don't know their names," I said. "They are for each of you, and you can give them any names you choose."

"For us?" asked Bluma. She seemed afraid to reach out and touch the dolls. But Becky grabbed one at once. "Her name is Dossi!" she shouted. "Little Dossi and you are Big Dossi."

"Then mine shall be Ruthi," said Bluma, taking hold of the other doll. "Little Ruthi."

Ruthi laughed aloud at Bluma's announcement and hugged the sisters. Their happiness was more contagious than diphtheria, and Ruthi had caught their joy.

So now there are two Dossis and two Ruthis in our building. But much more important, there are two very happy little girls and a woman who has regained her interest in life. Meyer may know the formulas for preparing medicines, but I found the recipe to cure my sister. I know she'll never forget Rosa, just as we'll never forget Mama and Papa and little Velvel. But one can't spend all the day mourning. Life must go on, and I'm so excited that it will. Just a few more months until the baby is born. Will it be a boy or a girl?

Love,
Big Dossi

To all my dear friends in Jericho, Vermont

Happy spring greetings during your Easter holiday!

Your New York friend,
Dossi

Dear Emma,

Since my last letter, we have celebrated the Jewish holiday of Passover. This is an annual festival. It takes place in the spring, but like all Jewish holidays, the days are settled by the lunar calendar and so it occurs on a different date each year, similar to your Easter celebration.

The holiday period lasts eight days and celebrates the Hebrews leaving ancient Egypt, where they were enslaved. Their journey with Moses to freedom is described in the biblical book of Exodus. Because the Jews departed so quickly, they did not have time for their bread to rise properly. So during this holiday,

Jewish people do not eat any leavened bread. Instead, we consume matzohs, which are like plain, flat crackers. In order to avoid all contact with leavening, we even have special sets of dishes that are used only during this eight-day period.

The holiday always begins with a family dinner called the Seder. Various prayers are recited, and the story of the holiday is read from a book called the Haggadah. In fact, the Seder is repeated two nights in a row. As I've told you before, Ruthi and I (and Meyer, too) are not always so observant of the old customs. And yet there are certain ones we feel compelled to follow because of our memories of Mama and Papa and the celebrations we shared in the past.

Last year Ruthi and I sat at the Seder table in the home of our former landlady on both evenings. Her husband led the readings, and her many children called out and cried so much that the experience was quite unpleasant. "I think God will understand if we skip the Seder next year," Ruthi whispered to me when it was over. "I have a headache and I'm sure those children gave God a headache, too."

We giggled at the blasphemy of those words and never guessed that this year we would live elsewhere and have another invitation. Meyer's old aunt and uncle sent us a letter asking us to spend the eve of Passover with them. They live uptown, and so we traveled by trolley. I carried a huge bag filled with fresh fruit that Ruthi had sent me out to buy. "I would have liked to bring a pot of soup," Ruthi said as the three of us set out together. "But I'm afraid it would wash the floor of the trolley long before we arrived at our destination."

The senior Reismans live on the west side of Manhattan, not too far from the Hudson River. Their apartment is very elegant, with pictures on the walls and rugs underfoot. "Someday you and I will live in an apartment like this, too," I heard Meyer whisper to Ruthi. I wonder where he thinks I will be then?

There were other guests as well—two cousins of Mrs. Reisman's and some other people whose relationship to one another I never figured out. I was the youngest in the room, and Ruthi was the next youngest. (We won't count the baby yet!) The words we recited and the order of the service are exactly the same in every home that celebrates this event. And yet, the contrast with the Seders of last year was amazing. In a way, it represented the contrast with my entire life. Who would have believed from one year to another there would be so many changes in my life? This year we observed the ritual of the second Seder at our own table on Allen Street. More soup, a roast, matzoh, and more traditional reading of the history of our people.

Since Jews do not eat any leavened bread for eight days following the Seder, Jewish charities distribute many thousands of pounds of free matzohs to help poorer people follow this observance. Last year Ruthi and I took advantage of this gift to stretch our small food budget rather than to be good observant Jews. But this year I've worked hard to eat no bread even though we could easily afford to buy it. It's a bigger mitzvah (good deed) not to eat fresh bread when you can afford to buy it than when you limit yourself to matzoh only because it's free and saves you the expense of buying the bread to fill your stomach. Just now my mouth is craving a slice of soft bread. I'm happy to report that tomorrow I'll be able to eat some with a clear conscience.

Your friend,
Dossi

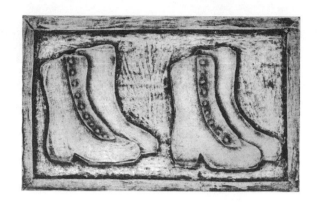

Dear Emma,

Remember how I wrote to you that Miss Wald said good would come out of the tragedy of the Triangle Fire? Well, already one good thing has occurred. Yesterday was Sunday, and Mimi came knocking at our door. Her mother gave her a rare morning off from her child-care chores. The two of us went walking together. We went to Tompkins Square Park, a much smaller place than the big Central Park I've written about before, but also much closer to our home. We sat together on a bench in the sun and Mimi told me her news.

The fire so upset her mother, who knew several of the victims, that she is determined that Mimi will not work in any clothing factory.

"What will you do?" I asked Mimi. I was afraid she was thinking of another type of employment, like becoming a housemaid who would clean for some rich people or a nursemaid caring for the children of a wealthy family.

"I will do nothing but go to school, at least for another year," Mimi said, smiling at me.

"You will do nothing but Latin verbs and calculus, read Shakespeare's plays and learn elocution and biology and botany and . . ."

"That's right," said Mimi, laughing. "Nothing at all."

She explained that her mother figured out that if they charged their boarder an extra dollar a week and if Mimi took in some sort of piecework that she could do evenings and on the weekend, they would be able to manage.

"I feel like the sloth we saw at the zoo last fall compared to you," I told her.

"You help Ruthi and you study hard and someday you will work harder than I can even imagine," Mimi said to make me feel better. During lunch at school I had told her about meeting Lillian Wald. And I revealed my conversation and thoughts about going to medical school. Mimi's dream is to get married and to live in an apartment with no one but her husband and her own children. "No boarders," she says. "That is my fantasy."

"A private bathroom," I suggest. There are so many things one can wish for but probably never attain.

"Meat every night of the week," Mimi added to the list.

"A different dress to wear each day."

"Two pairs of shoes, so if I get caught in the rain, I can put on dry ones."

We went on and on, and our fantasies got wilder and wilder: a ride in an automobile; a ride in an aeroplane, I suggested, topping her dream.

"A trip across the country to see all forty-six states," said Mimi, attempting to top me once again. We laughed and laughed at all these incredible possibilities. But the truth is, I don't want a ride in an aeroplane or a trip across the United States. I will be very happy if I make another trip as far as Jericho, Vermont, so that I can visit with you and your family.

I think that is my fantasy for now. Ruthi insists she can manage on her own after the baby is born. But it is still too soon to tell. After all, she's never been a mother before.

Love,
Dossi

Dear Emma,

As I wrote the date on this letter, I got gooseflesh. It's exactly two months since the horrible Triangle fire. I wonder if the number twenty-five will continue to have that effect on me for years to come. A few times recently, I've walked past the Asch Building, where the fire occurred. The building gives off a horrid, damp, smokey odor that turns my stomach. How ironic that the building has the name that it does! But most recently, I saw that they were tearing out the old wood and beginning to repair the damage. I don't believe in ghosts, but I think if I ever worked at that site, I would feel haunted by the memory of the past and would have visions of 146 young women hovering over my head as I tried to concentrate.

On a much happier note, do you remember last summer when I told you about the enormous library that was being built in the city? Well, after several years of work, the library is finally completed. On Tuesday it was officially dedicated. I wasn't there, but I read about it yesterday in Meyer's newspaper. Hundreds of important people were invited to the official opening ceremonies. Even President Taft came from Washington to make a speech. Yesterday, which was the first day that the new library was open to the general public, fifty thousand people visited it. The library will be open every day of the year, even Sundays and holidays. I am eager to get inside and see it for myself.

Now that the warm spring weather is finally here, I'll probably get to the Central Park Menagerie again. In the meantime, I've taken to going on shorter walking expeditions with Ruthi whenever I can. Meyer says that the exercise is good for her, but I can't understand why. Still, I enjoy having this private time with her. Too soon she will be occupied with the baby.

Yesterday as we walked down the stairs, Bluma and Becky were just leaving their apartment. I could see their mother was holding a large bundle, and I guessed she was going off to deliver some of the piece-work she does at home. Mrs. Edelman looked at Ruthi and smiled. "Not too much longer?" she asked, referring to the baby. (Now that Ruthi isn't wearing a coat, it's very obvious to everyone that she is expecting a child shortly.)

"Just another few weeks," Ruthi said, blushing.

"God willing, you'll have a son," Mrs. Edelman said. "And an easy delivery."

Ruthi blushed again. "A boy, a girl. As long as the child's healthy," she responded.

We went on our way and I said to Ruthi, "How can she say that to you: *'God willing, you'll have a son'?* It sounds as if having a daughter is not just as important. She has two daughters. Does she wish they were boys?"

Ruthi shrugged. "People seem to think that there's a bigger honor attached to the birth of a son. There is someone to say Kaddish when you die, for example." (*Kaddish* is the prayer that Jewish men recite in memory of the deceased.)

"Well, why can't a woman recite those prayers?" I asked angrily.

Ruthi laughed at me. "Don't scold me. I didn't

make up the traditions," she said.

After that, I suddenly became aware of how many people stopped Ruthi. Some touched her stomach for good luck. Others said things like, "May you have ten sons," or "I wish you a handsome boy."

When we stopped to buy a piece of fish to cook for supper at one of the stalls along Orchard Street, the vendor said, "Don't forget to send someone to me when you need fish to serve at the *bris mila.*" (That's another Jewish custom, and it occurs on the eighth day after the birth of a boy. There isn't any ceremony for a girl!)

"If she has a daughter, I'm coming straight back here and buying a piece of fish to make a party for her," I said sharply.

"Good. Good. Just be sure to shop here," the man said.

I looked at the man in his dirty apron, covered with fish blood and scales, and thought, Why am I angry at him? His hands were rough, with cracked nails and cuts from his work. I wondered if he had a son, but I didn't ask.

"Doesn't it bother you?" I asked Ruthi as we walked away.

"That people want me to have a son?"

"Yes. After all, if Mama had only sons, neither you nor I would be walking along the street together."

"You're right," she said. "And the truth is, the world could not exist without women. So let them say what they want. I really don't care. I know they mean well."

"Oh, Ruthi. You are so good natured. I can never be like you," I said, hugging her. Then I had another thought. "Do you think Meyer wants a son so badly?" I asked.

"He would be pleased to have a boy to name after his father. But he won't be unhappy if we have a daughter."

I wondered about the other child, the baby that was stillborn when his first wife died. Was it a boy or a girl? But I didn't want to ask Ruthi that question. Better not to think about dead babies.

So here we are, waiting for the baby. Fortunately, I have so many final exams to take that my head doesn't dwell on the waiting or the sex of the unborn baby. I've been bringing my autograph album to school every day lately. Many of my classmates will be going to different schools in the fall, and still more, as I've told you, will not continue their formal education at all. Even though we all live in the same neighborhood, we may never cross paths again. The lines we write in one another's albums will be a final reminder of these friendships. This is what my teacher, Miss Clark, wrote in my book yesterday:

May tender hands be guiding thee
Where'er thou mayest go.
The truest joy betiding thee,
That any life can know.

I was very moved by her warm sentiment until I discovered that she wrote the same words to every student who gave her an album to sign.

Love,
Dossi

P.S. I am looking forward to receiving your letter describing your brother's wedding. Don't leave out a single detail!

June 25, 1911

Dear Emma,

I have so much news to report, but I shall begin at the beginning and tell it to you step by step, as it occurred.

Yesterday was graduation day at my school. It was also graduation day at all of the other elementary schools throughout the city. In my school alone there were 117 students who had completed eighth grade. I know you will gasp at that number. After all, you've told me there are only eleven boys and girls in the one-room school that you attend. But 117 is only a small fraction of the number of students in all of New York City who have passed the exams signifying the completion of eighth grade this year.

There was a ceremony held at the school, and the boys were told to wear dark trousers and white shirts. Girls were to wear dark skirts and white middy blouses with navy ties. Of course, not everyone could afford such outfits. But somehow, by borrowing from friends and relatives, the majority were properly attired. And so was I. I wore Ruthi's navy skirt, and she had made me a middy blouse and tie for the occasion. Those students who were not wearing the right clothes were seated behind others during the graduation ceremony.

Each student was permitted to invite two guests. Of course, Ruthi and Meyer were my guests. I looked for them as we stood ready to march into the school auditorium. But there were so many people that I couldn't see them. Parents and other relatives, friends, and infants filled the auditorium seats. (Apparently mothers insisted that since babies did not need a seat, they were not included in the two-guest ruling. There were more small children than graduates and more crying than singing during the morning!)

Miss Marshall, one of the sixth-grade teachers, played the piano as we graduates marched to our seats. We were told to keep our eyes focused on the head in front of us and not to speak. But everyone, including me, turned to seek out their guests. It was our last day at school, and so no one had to worry about a mark for poor conduct or inappropriate behavior on our report cards. Still, as we entered the auditorium, the solemnity of the occasion took over. It was quite wonderful to know that all of us had come this far. Only a small handful of my fellow graduates had been born in America. Only a very few knew English as their first language.

When we were seated on the auditorium stage, I could look out directly at the audience. Still, I couldn't locate Ruthi or Meyer. I stood when the color guard marched down the aisle with two flags, one American and one blue and gold for the City of New York. I sang two patriotic songs and bowed my head as Mr. Charles, the school principal, read a psalm from the Bible. Some awards were given out, and I'm proud to report that I received two. First was a certificate for excellent attendance during the year, and second and more important was a prize for best achievement. I was given a fountain pen, and I am using it now and will be doing so for all my future letters to you. Finally, we were awarded our diplomas. Each name was called out individually, and because the names were in alphabetical order, I had a long wait until Mr. Charles reached *R,* but I sat turning my new pen over and over in my fingers.

By the time I heard *Hadassah Rabinowitz,* I had searched the entire audience and decided that Ruthi and Meyer were not there. I didn't know if I should be hurt because they had forgotten to come or worried that something had befallen them. When all the diplomas had been distributed, I hugged Mimi and one or two other girls and hurried off for home.

As I raced up the stairs of my house, Mrs. Edelman stopped me. "The midwife came a little while ago. But I don't think the baby has come yet."

"The baby! The baby!" I cried out, and ran as fast as I could up the next flight. The baby wasn't due for another couple of weeks.

When I entered our apartment, I saw Meyer, looking pale and anxious. There was also a tall, gray-haired woman who I had never seen before. And on the bed in the next room was my sister. Meyer and the midwife refused to let me enter. "But I'm Ruthi's sister," I told the tall woman, who was blocking me from the door.

"You'll see your sister later," she told me. "She

doesn't need company now."

I turned to Meyer, hoping he would tell the midwife to let me go to Ruthi.

"Perhaps it would be all right if we took a walk?" he asked the midwife instead.

"A fine idea," she exclaimed. "Husbands are always in the way. And younger sisters are just as bad."

I tried to resist, but I was outnumbered. Meyer took me by the arm and led me to the door. "Everything will be fine," he promised me, his words sounding more certain than his tone. "Perhaps the baby will be here when we get back?" he said hopefully, turning to the midwife.

"That depends on how far you walk," she retorted, and then went into Ruthi's room, closing the door behind her.

Meyer and I walked down the street. It was a warm and sunny day, and the streets seemed filled with mothers and babies. Soon Ruthi, too, would be out walking with a new baby, I thought happily. Then I looked at Meyer.

"Are you very nervous?" I asked him.

"It doesn't seem fair that a woman has to go through the entire birth process on her own," he said.

"But Ruthi is healthy and strong. She had an easy pregnancy. She should be fine."

Something in his tone made me feel that he was saying those words to reassure himself more than me.

"Yes," I agreed, hoping to make him feel better. "Ruthi will be fine. And the baby, too."

"And the baby, too," Meyer echoed.

At the corner Meyer steered me toward the right, and I realized we were walking toward the pharmacy where he works.

"I never said it, but you must know how grateful I am that you helped Ruthi after the fire," he said as we walked along. "She was so upset. And I felt so helpless. I don't know how Ruthi would have gotten through that awful time without you."

I felt myself blushing at his unexpected praise.

"Do you want a boy?" I asked him, changing the subject.

"We both, Ruthi and I, want a healthy baby. Sex doesn't matter at all," he said, and I knew he was sincere.

"Good," I said.

We arrived at the pharmacy and went in. I do like the shop. It has shelves with large bottles filled with colored liquids or powders. Each bottle can do something to help a sick person. I know they carry bicarbonate of soda for upset stomachs, aspirin, and special elixirs to control pain. The store also sells toiletry items like soaps, tooth powder, and scented toilet water. I like the mixture of odors that one can smell in that shop. Behind the counter stood old Mr. Conovitz, the owner and Meyer's boss.

"What news do you have?" he asked eagerly. But of course, we didn't have anything to report.

"I just had to get out of the apartment," Meyer said, sighing.

Mr. Conovitz nodded his head in understanding.

"You've met my sister-in-law, Dossi, before, haven't you?" Meyer asked the old man.

"Of course." Mr. Conovitz smiled at me. He walked into the back room and returned with a paper cone filled with peppermints. "Here, young lady," he said. "You look quite splendid in that outfit of yours."

I looked down and noticed my middy blouse and tie. Only then did I remember that less than an hour before I had graduated from grammar school. It seemed like something that had happened days or weeks ago.

Meyer suddenly remembered, too. "Yes, indeed," he said to Mr. Conovitz. "Today was a big day for Dossi. It was the school graduation, and Ruthi and I were planning to attend. But there was an unexpected interruption in our plans. Dossi is a bright girl," he added. "Too bad she isn't a boy. We could offer her a job here when she finishes school."

"I could still work," I said. "It doesn't matter that I'm a girl."

Meyer put his hand on my shoulder. "Girls are made to become mothers," he said. "But I approve of your education. You'll be able to help your sons do their homework someday."

I was about to begin an argument with him when I realized I didn't want to spoil this day with debates about work for women. No, I won't ever work in the pharmacy, but it won't be because I'm a female. I'll become a doctor and prescribe medicines that Meyer can make up in the pharmacy for my patients. And perhaps through my work, I'll be able to help cure children with diphtheria, influenza, pneumonia, scarlet fever, or whooping cough. Won't Meyer be surprised by that?

We stayed at the shop a little longer and then we

left to return to the apartment.

"Be sure and let me know the news," Mr. Conovitz called to us. "Perhaps I'll have to clean my suit for the *bris mila* ceremony."

So there was another person who waited for a son, I thought, making a face. We hurried back to the apartment, stopping only to buy a bouquet of spring flowers and a loaf of fresh bread and some pot cheese for our lunch.

Now, Emma. Here's the big news. When we got back to the house, Mrs. Edelman was waiting by her door. "Hurry, hurry," she said, beaming.

Obviously, she had not done a stitch of sewing all morning if she was keeping track of events in the apartment above her head! Meyer and I ran up the stairs. He pushed the door open, and there stood the midwife holding a tiny bundle in her arms.

"How is Ruthi?" Meyer asked, not even looking at the baby. If ever I knew that he loved my sister, that was certainly the moment. And I forgave him for putting down the female sex just a little while ago and for every one of our quarrels in the past.

"She's fine. She's resting," the midwife said. "This little thing just slid out without much effort. She was eager to join the world. She doesn't know what's in store for her."

"*She?*" I asked.

"She," the midwife said. "I judge that she weighs about six pounds."

Meyer turned to look at his daughter. His eyes were full of tears of joy. He licked his lips and cleared his throat. He was too moved to speak. But finally, he said, "Well, Aunt Dossi. What do you think of your niece?"

The midwife let me hold the baby. Do you remember holding Nell when she was an infant? It wouldn't be the same thing because you were still so young yourself. The baby opened her eyes. "She's looking at me," I squealed with delight.

Instantly the eyes closed again. "She can't see anything yet," the midwife explained.

"She looked. And she saw me," I said. I was convinced.

Later, when Ruthi was sitting up in bed, she told me the name of this newest member of our family. "She's Sarah Rose," she said. I knew that my niece was bearing the names of both our mother and my sister's dear friend. Neither will ever have the joy of seeing and holding her, but the arrival of this new being eases a little the ache from the losses of those whose names she has taken on. *Sarah Rose.*

Love,
Aunt Dossi

July 3, 1911

Dear Emma,

Sarah Rose is a placid and happy baby. She sleeps and eats and sleeps with hardly a whimper in between. We're fortunate that she does not have colic like all the children of our former landlady, Mrs. Aronson. A new baby at her home meant no sleep, not just for the mother and infant, but for their family and for all of us boarders as well.

The baby has performed one amazing feat already: somehow she has managed to change her double name into a shorter, simpler one. One by one, we've taken to calling this little darling Sally.

"I have no question that I can manage Sally on my

own," Ruthi said to me yesterday.

"Are you certain?" I asked. I looked toward Meyer. What did he have to say about this?

"Very certain," Ruthi said, and Meyer nodded his head in agreement.

And so it is decided. I will stay close to home and help Ruthi for the remainder of July. But on the first of August, I will be boarding the train to Jericho, Vermont, just as I did a year ago. I am excited at the thought of seeing you and all your family. I am eager to meet your new sister-in-law and to admire the dresses that you and Nell wore to the wedding. (I can't believe that you've saved a piece of the wedding cake in the icehouse for me!)

It occurs to me that although we're no longer the strangers to each other that we were a year ago, in some ways you will be meeting a new person. After all, so much has happened, both good and bad, during the months since we were last together, that I am not exactly the same person as the one to whom you said good-bye last summer. But then, neither are you the same person. We change all the time. Ruthi measured me and discovered that I've grown three inches since last summer. She says my face looks more mature, too. But of course, it's the internal change that I'm really thinking of. Isn't it good that we've had our correspondence to help us share the thoughts and ideas that have passed through our heads during the last ten months?

I'm looking forward to eating your mother's buttermilk pancakes with Vermont maple syrup. I'm looking forward to another lesson in cow milking. But most of all, I am looking forward to being with you and all your family.

Hugs and love to you all,
Dossi

Author's Note

Perhaps you met Dossi Rabinowitz in *Faraway Summer,* when she spent two weeks as a guest at the home of Emma Meade in Jericho, Vermont. The year was 1910, and Dossi had never been so far away before. Now she is back home again on New York City's Lower East Side, and it's my chance to tell you about her life there.

This is a book of fiction. I have invented Dossi and her sister and friends. But everything else in this book is true. No author could invent the poverty and hard times that thousands and thousands of immigrants endured during the early days of the twentieth century. Yet despite the hardships, more and more people continued to cross the ocean to live in the New World. For difficult as life was here, they were escaping from much worse: enforced inscription in the army, extreme poverty and starvation, and very limited chances for education and employment. Russian Jews also faced pogroms where hundreds of people were attacked and murdered for no reason other than their religion. And so the people kept on coming.

Diphtheria, the disease that Bluma and Becky contract, was once the killer of about fifteen thousand individuals, mostly children, each year. At the turn of the twentieth century, diphtheria, tuberculosis, scarlet fever, whooping cough, and many other diseases put life at risk for infants and young children. Many, many did not grow to adulthood. The fact that these diseases have been essentially conquered by mandatory vaccination in our country and are now only to be read about in medical books, history books, and historical fiction gives us encouragement to believe that someday there will be an end to cancer and AIDS.

No author could have so morbid and sadistic an imagination as to create the horror of the mass death that resulted from the Triangle Shirtwaist Factory fire, which actually occurred on March 25, 1911, when 146 women died either from the flames and smoke or by jumping out of windows. I created Rosa, but all her coworkers really existed and really lost their lives. It was as a direct result of that tragedy that the building regulations and safety codes that we take for granted nowadays began to be enacted.

And, finally, although I created her conversations in this book, I did not invent Lillian Wald. This amazing woman, who founded the Visiting Nurse Service of New York, which continues to this day, really did exist and devoted her life and resources to helping the poor, sick people of the Lower East Side of New York City. It was the beginning of social service in this country, and she left a legacy of concern and efforts for others to build on.

I learned about the period 1910–11 by reading both old issues of *The New York Times* from those years, which are stored in libraries on microfilm, and from articles that are available on the Internet. I read many books: nonfiction studies, autobiographical accounts of the early 1900s, and even fiction. And I looked at hundreds of photographs and visited the Lower East Side Tenement Museum, which has re-created the living spaces of the past. All this transported me to that earlier time.

I hope from reading this book you, too, will be transported to that other time and place. It was a bad period, but there was much good, too. It was an era with amazing change: the telephone, automobiles, and even aeroplanes (as they were then called) were each coming into their own. Workers were clamoring for more money and better working conditions. Women were still demanding the right to vote. It would be coming soon. Life would never be the same again. It was the last decade before World War I, a war that changed our sensibilities and awareness of America's relationship to the rest of the world.

In 1911, when there were still few telephones and the advent of e-mail was beyond the imagination of any scientist or science fiction writer, families and friends kept in touch by writing letters. Mail traveled across the country by train and across the ocean on steamships. In those days it cost two cents to buy a postage stamp to send a letter from New York City to Jericho, Vermont. Once posted, it would take only one or two days for the letter to arrive. Two friends like Dossi and Emma, without the distraction of television and computer games, car rides, and shopping malls, would write frequently and share their news and thoughts. The act of writing a letter, like the act of receiving and reading one, would serve as an excellent recreation and would strengthen their friendship. Out in the country in the early years of the twentieth century, the isolation of rural America was broken when horsedrawn buggies, early cars (and in winter, sleds) began delivering cards, letters, newspapers, and mail-order catalogs directly to the homes of farmers. Rural Free Delivery (called RFD for short) meant that the long trip to the post office was no longer necessary in order to receive mail.

Letters received from friends and family were read, and reread, and then saved and treasured by the recipients. The handwriting in these letters was usually beautifully elegant because these letters were written in an era when penmanship was an important classroom subject and a skill to be admired. There were no ballpoint pens or markers. Writers used pens that they dipped into a bottle of ink. Fountain pens that held a reservoir of ink were a new innovation. Newspaper advertisements from 1910 offered such pens for $3.50, more money than most people could afford to spend for such a luxury item. You may discover letters from this time bundled together in old trunks in attics, and in antiques shops and flea markets around the country. But you won't find any from Dossi Rabinowitz to Emma Meade. Those letters are only to be found inside this book.